Praise f

PEN Trar
Winner of t
Shortlisted XVI Dulce Chacón Novel Award
Shortlisted New Spanish Books 2021 - UK and French
Panel's Choice

'In a flaunt of Cervantine metafiction, Mora projects
onto the reader his thoughts on truth and verisimilitude.'
- ABC

'Impeccable, from beginning to end.'
- Carlos Zanón, *El País*

'A text perfectly in line with our times'
- CTXT

'Mora embarks on a radical adventure in a Europe ravaged
by wars and revolutions that has no reference in our current literature.'
- La Vanguardia

A catalogue record for this book is available from the British Library

First published in English in 2023 by Peninsula Press

400 Kingsland Road
E8 4AA
London
peninsulapress.co.uk

Cover design by Theo Inglis

Artwork by Javier Hirschfeld

Typesetting by Geethik Technologies

Printed in the UK by CPI Group (UK) Ltd., Croydon

ISBN-13: 9781913512392

2 4 6 8 10 9 7 5 3 1

Translated from Spanish by Rahul Bery. Support for the translation of this
book was provided by Acción Cultural Española, AC/E.

This book has been selected to receive financial assistance from English PEN's
PEN Translates programme, supported by Arts Council England. English
PEN exists to promote literature and our understanding of it, to uphold
writers' freedoms around the world, to campaign against the persecution and
imprisonment of writers for stating their views, and to promote the friendly
co-operation of writers and the free exchange of ideas. www.englishpen.org

Centroeuropa

Vicente Luis Mora

Translated by Rahul Bery

PENINSULA PRESS, LONDON

To Helena Cortés Gabaudan, with gratitude

For Virginia

But, the reader will say, is this a guide to Germany or a mere novella you are proposing I read?

STENDHAL, *The Pink and the Green* (1837)

The people at the top are again busy making world-history.

T. FONTANE, *Before the storm* (1878)

Through all the solitudes, through ocean-wide chaos, she has brought me back again to land!

J.W. VON GOETHE, *Faust* (II, 1832)

1

Male, Prussian, hussar soldier, frozen.

That was the first body I found while digging in the frozen earth to bury my wife; I say *my wife* because I never knew her real name, although I will return to that later.

When one finds a buried body under one's own earth, in one's own soil, one suspects it is not alone; in some way, anyone who finds a corpse fears or suspects that other corpses are out there, waiting their turn. The fields of a given place cannot be looked at in the same way once the first body has been found, for now they no longer resemble flower meadows but burial grounds.

The story began with the discovery of that first soldier, but what I wish to write cannot be properly understood unless I go back a few hours to my anguished interview with Mayor Altmayer. Or perhaps I should go further and recall those sad days in Mainz? I ask the potential reader to forgive me for faltering as I expound, for these memories constitute the first long text I have ever put to paper, and the past is so wide, long, and deep, that choosing any single part as a starting point constitutes, in some way, an imposture. Nothing starts at an exact point. Our lives do not start entirely with our births.

Yes, I will recount in detail the tense conversation I had with Mayor Altmayer on the day of my move to Oderburch, shortly after first looking upon the river Oder and seeing its splendid silver ambling idly towards the north; I must relate my talk with that official, during which I began to discern the complexities of that time in the third decade of the century I arrived here, dates I cannot recall with any precision because my wife and I lived too much in the present and every day was the same to us, happy and identical, identically happy, until she died, and they became unhappy and interchangeable, interchangeably miserable once I lost her in Mainz, that baneful city where my beloved vanished forever.

I will recount all of it, certainly, but be patient, for before I begin my tale you must first allow me to recall the stupefaction that overcame me when, digging into the soil in my newly acquired plot of earth – a few cultivable acres by the river, which flowed remorselessly, like a shot from a rifle – I unearthed the surprised, frozen face of that young, almost childlike Prussian soldier, with an additional button on his cassock at heart height, festooned with blood; imagine my surprise, no less great than yours, as I unearthed him, staring straight into his sparkling, wide-open eyes as I dug from that hard surface the six feet of Prussian earth which I had been planning to give to my beautiful wife as a first and final wedding present, inasmuch as her grim dowry was to consist of cartloads of melancholy, of which I would freely dispose over many years, right to this day, upon which I have sat down to write out these recollections, to put them in order; and for that reason I must unearth all of these memories, in case they might be of use to someone, perhaps a historian like my faithful Jakob Moltke, my cherished first teacher and then friend, to whom I owe so much, and to whom I would like to dedicate this document, for reasons that will be understood shortly. I digress again, but I want to demonstrate to the unlikely reader of this document the perplexity which I, Redo Hauptshammer, born in a Vienna brothel at some point during the death throes of the 18th century, felt as I went to bury my wife one frozen morning and found, in my new and not very large tillage field, the corpse of that frozen soldier, watching me unmoved as if his death in battle had occurred at that very moment, as if he were freshly fallen, an unexpected guest in the kingdom of shadows, just as I was a fresh arrival in the kingdom of Frederick William III of Prussia; and, spade in hand, I recalled Mayor Altmayer's words, 'You'll have problems out there, next to the Oder, for when you dig deep you will doubtless find water,' and I realised, on only my second day in the Oderbruch, that, in those history-scarred lands, no sooner do you open up the ground than you find deep rivers of blood.

2

One is unaware of what to expect along the way, and surprised by the way life intones two melodies at once: sombre and even more sombre. These harmonic lines are soon joined by another, making three, and then others, those of the disasters and errors yet to be perpetrated, like voices in a chorus. My wife Odra (not her real name) and I knew this from that fateful 4th of August when we had decided to leave Vienna and put our 'French plan' into action. The idea was to spend five months in France, the motives for which I will recount later, with the intention of acquainting ourselves with agricultural work, preparing the foundations of our social act and looking ahead to what our future together in Szonden might bring. And though we are now approaching the narration of these tales – in the same way that I was approaching Szonden after a sorrowful six-day journey, counting from the horrible incident in Mainz – allow me to add that one's luck can change suddenly, without explanation, which is what happened when, mere days later, I found two more Napoleonic soldiers buried together as I was excavating my small plot for the second time in search of a suitable place to bury Odra's coffin. And all this from nowhere, for these momentous events occurred in that same fortnight between our entering Mainz together, after our period spent in France, and my sad, solitary arrival in Szonden; life had lacerated my heart by robbing me of my most beloved, and yet, ironically, it had also almost simultaneously endowed me with the means to sustain myself for the rest of my days.

I reached Oderbruch after crossing eight counties of the old March of Brandenburg; I knew that Szonden, the small village where the portion of earth that would form my new home could be found, was located on the edge of the Oder, the wide river which separates the Old March from the New, not far from Frankfurt von Oder, almost halfway between Berlin and the formerly Polish city of Kostrzyn. Szonden is such a small place that its name was and is only known in the immediate surroundings, which meant I had to ask for Frankfurt or Lebus to find my way; my horse was showing signs of exhaustion after the lengthy journey, one entire day plus nine hours' travel from Magdeburg, the last place in which we had rested upon a common bed of straw, dragging myself and the wagon; and the wagon was a fair weight, both physically and materially, since it carried many belongings and bales, not to mention the casket containing Odra.

When we saw the first houses of what appeared to be Szonden, I got down from the driving seat and removed the snow-covered cloth from the coffin, in case the sight of it could work as a decisive argument in what I imagined would be an arduous exchange with Mayor Altmayer; I remember that moment of fatigue and excitement as if it were happening right before my eyes; the partially frozen river Oder ten cubits to my right; the snow-covered road; the shivers I felt, whether from the deep winter cold or from the closeness to Odra's casket, I do not know; the awareness that everything I had imagined could come to grief; the knowledge that nothing could get worse.

My nerves overcame me to such an extent that I decided to sit down in order to quell my thoughts, doing so upon the coarse coffin containing my beloved, the lid of which, having been covered, was the only warm place to hand; to calm myself I repeated those words – which I needed to absorb down to my deepest core – eleven times out loud: *My name is Redo Hauptshammer and I was born in Vienna to an Austrian mother and an unknown father;* I also paid attention to the tone in which I uttered them, because I could not let my desperation give me away and make all the plans I had carefully dreamt up with Odra go to ruin; when I opened my eyes, there was a giant towering over me, staring blankly at me.

Slender as an arquebus, his lower teeth on view in his open mouth and with eyes that betrayed his meagre intelligence, this curiosity was so tall that his face was level with mine even though I was sitting on a casket which was itself upon a wagon; the colossus must have measured at least twelve feet; 'I am Udo,' he said, and I understood that he was responding to my previous litany, repeating my name to convince myself of it, to make the name and surname mine, and since I was already in my new country, I changed my tone of voice. *I believe the houses that can be seen from here announce the village of Szonden;* 'It is certain that we are in Szonden'; *I would be very grateful to you if you could bring me before the mayor; Altmayer; is that the mayor's name?*; 'Mayor Altmayer. It is exactly thirteen minutes past one.' I did not understand, his look was abject, I thought he was completely mad until he made an unnerving comment: 'There is something strange about you.'

I couldn't be found out that easily, not after almost three years' training with Odra, after easily passing the test of mixing with all kinds of people over a period of several months in France; it was completely unthinkable that an idiot would lift the veil of my careful disguise after less than three utterances, and I was soothed by the thought that it must have been my Austrian accent which the giant found disconcerting, for I was still a foreigner, a new arrival in a new reality; in fact, the following day I remembered the moment of horror I experienced just before Udo took me to number 14, Oderstrasse, the property of Mayor Altmayer; I remembered it after reburying Frederick William II's hussar – a detail which was revealed to me by my friend Jakob – which I had brought to light while attempting to bury my dear Odra. Perhaps the memory of Udo was provoked by the long shadow of one of the fifteen cypresses separating my farm from that of Hans, the neighbouring farmer, for it was next to that row of trees that I decided to begin the new inhumation, which ended up being another exhumation; such was my surprise when, once again, I found a trail of coagulated blood, and then, a cubit further down, hit my spade against something very hard after digging with all my strength; the object was so hard I suspected it might be a buried chest, full of coins perhaps; I wondered if the local laws, of which I knew nothing, would attribute ownership, in such a circumstance, to the finder.

I was already imagining a new conversation with Altmayer about this outcome, after our lengthy talk the day before – to which, I suppose, this story will soon turn – when I discovered with horror that the supposed gold chest was in fact a human body, *another* human body; after some considerable effort, and the extraction of around sixteen cubic metres of earth and slush, I not only exhumed the entire body, but a second cadaver, buried next to it; two twin brothers, dressed in Napoleonic uniforms, with bullet and bayonet wounds in several regions of their completely frozen bodies. I struggled to contain my tears, since a companion of these infantrymen had mistakenly caused the death of my Odra in Mainz; that is why Jakob's subsequent explanation was not needed: French uniforms, together with Austrian ones from after 1790, were the only ones I could remember; in despair I sat down by the huge open hole, sweating from the effort despite the implausible cold of that foggy morning, facing two identical bodies sleeping their eternal slumber while my wife's coffin, which I had dragged with much difficulty to this end of the field, looked at me perplexed; in case that wasn't enough, it began to snow again.

I realised that I couldn't stay out in the elements for too long, sweaty as I was, without running the risk of pneumonia, an illness I could not allow for, since I depended on my own hands for my survival, so I gathered all my strength and began digging some eighteen paces away, almost by the path at which the western edge of my land ends; I dug with a mixture of fatigue, sorrow and desperation, which only grew when I made the second discovery, but I will turn to that new aberration later, as

I believe it is finally time to return to the previous day, when the giant Udo had left me at the door outside a beautiful house in Szonden, where a man was waiting with his arms crossed and looking at us sternly, in defiance of the unbelievable cold: Mayor Altmayer.

3

I am conscious of my promise to transcribe the conversation with Altmayer, whom we have only just met at his doorstep, frowning and dressed with Prussian elegance; but my inexperience when it comes to constructing such a long, eventful tale, invites me to freeze Mayor Altmayer for a moment, standing there before his typical white *Giebelhaus* with its pointed tiles and dark wood, because I want to relate, so that I don't forget, a detail I judge to be important and which I will surely neglect if I get too immersed in recounting my tense conversation with our good mayor.

While crossing Magdeburg some days before, my wagon, loaded with goods, furniture, my beloved's coffin and several bundles of luggage – I still found it impossible to throw away Odra's clothes, though I knew she would never wear them again – I passed an enormous building with some connected warehouses on the outskirts of the city; at the gateway to the building a sign read COQUI, and I asked the street porters who were toiling outside why that building was the source of so much traffic of men and wagons. They told me it was the refinery that belonged to the powerful Coqui family, and that the objective of the large installations was to process sugar from beet, a herbaceous plant which, so they told me, was growing in popularity in various states of the old German Confederation. I entered a small shop which gave onto the main avenue and asked, with one eye on my belongings, how much the seeds cost. The price seemed reasonable and, after a brief negotiation, I acquired four big sacks, which I only just managed to lift onto my wagon, before continuing on my way.

I did not want these details to escape me, because numbers and details are relevant to this story. Now we can revive Mayor Altmayer, whom we have left frozen in time, so that he may express himself freely.

'This stranger is looking for you, Mayor Altmayer.' 'I can see that, Udo,' the mayor said, having observed my whinnying horse and laden wagon. 'It's too cold to talk out here, let's go in. Thank you, Udo.' 'You're welcome, Mayor Altmayer.' As I covered the horse, I admired the giant as he walked off, stooping over slightly. I looked for the folder that I had brought from France, hidden under the reins; holding it in my hands, my head liberated from my felt hat, I crossed the threshold of Mayor Altmayer's house, pleasantly warm from the chimney fire. The house was beautiful and glittering, with thick white walls and a line of bricks at the bottom. Unfortunately, we did not stay in the living room, where a silent and rotund woman – whom I did not yet know by her name, Genoveva Ulmer, and who was not introduced to me at that moment – was labouring by the fire, watching me from the corner of her eye; I was obliged to move into an adjoining and somewhat cooler office, into which the thin servant Utta silently carried a glowing stove. Altmayer sat behind the only table, moving pompously to lend himself authority, and as there was nowhere to sit I remained standing before him, prepared for the highly important conversation which was about to take place and which I had been imagining for months, like an actor rehearsing his part.

'Who are you and why have you come to Szonden?' I cleared my throat and began my performance, upon the success of which rested nothing less than my entire future: *My name is Redo Hauptshammer and I was born in Vienna to an Austrian mother and an unknown father. I have come to settle in Szonden alone* – at this point I sighed – *because my wife, who is in my wagon, confined in her coffin, died a few days ago in Mainz from the shots of an escaped French solder...* 'I'm sorry,' Altmayer interrupted, and I was sincerely grateful, although I said nothing, for my nerves were coiled around me like a snake around its prey. I continued, sounding somewhat rushed: *Thank you; as I was saying, this immense loss has truncated our plans, converting them into my plans only. Our initial idea was to settle here, on a small parcel of cultivable land that was given to me by mister Duisdorf.* Altmayer's eyes opened wide. 'Magnus Duisdorf?' *I think so; although I cannot read well, I can spell and recognise written words.* 'It could be Duisdorf. I knew him. He left Szonden suddenly a few years ago. He had problems,' Altmayer declared, as if he preferred not to talk. *He had them in Austria too,* I added, since it served my argument. 'That doesn't surprise me,' Altmayer responded drily. *My late wife used familial contacts to help that gentleman solve at least one major problem, I'm not sure exactly what; and in fair reciprocity, Duisdorf wanted to compensate her life-saving intervention with a small plot of land, the deeds to which I carry in this folder.* 'My my... That would be one of the first transfers of free land to occur in these fields since the government's agrarian reforms; until now no Einlieger has ever sold or given away their property. These are unprecedented times,' Altmayer added, and sat there for a moment looking at me, as if there was something strange or false about me, some imposture. Since that was indeed the case, although he could not and must not know it, I remained silent, controlling my nerves, holding back my voice so that it would not escape from my throat involuntarily, or proffer any inconsistencies that might give me away. But it was Altmayer who shouted: 'Utta!' Utta, the servant, came promptly, while Altmayer and I contemplated each other in frosty silence. 'Bring a chair for Mr... Sorry...' *Redo Haupsthammer.* 'I shall call you Redo, if you don't mind; as there is nobody else in the locality with that name, it will be easy to identify you.' Just like that, he placed me onto a lower rung, almost on the same level as the servants; a little later I learnt that it had been only a decade or so since the end of peasant feudalism in Prussia, and Altmayer had been slow to adapt to the new era, retaining much fondness and nostalgia for the previous one.

Utta brought the chair and I was about to sit on it when Altmayer stopped me with a gesture, teaching me the first lesson about the region's customs: when you are with someone who considers themselves superior to you, you do not sit until you have been given permission to do so. Then he said: 'I have no issue, in principle, with what you say; but since it is the first time and because it comes through Duisdorf, whose presence even as a ghost always complicates things, I beseech you to show me the deeds, so that I can examine their authenticity.' *Of course, Mr Altmayer, here they are. With them I pass you my destiny. It is in your hands now.* I added this so as not to undermine his imagined position of superiority, which seemed so important to him, and to incline him towards viewing me favourably. 'These papers are safe with me, Redo, do not worry. You may sit,' he added. I sat. As I knew the document well, for Odra and I had read it excitedly thousands of times, I could make out which parts his eyes came to rest upon; the land's classification, a cultivable plot with a hut built for living in; the size, a little more than two *Morgen* or acres, although I did not know what that measure amounted to in these parts, since they tended to differ throughout Europe; and finally, the most important thing: the names and seals of the people who gave their reliable testimony to the existence of the land and our corresponding right to ownership. The signatures and emblems of the Justice Minister, acting in the name of king Frederick William III, were visible; so were those of the prefect of the Oderbruch county and last of all, the rubric of Magnus Duisdorf, signed in his own hand: I cede these deeds and the corresponding property to Mr Redo Hauptshammer and his wife, Odra Churbredo, natives of Vienna and Madrid respectively, signed in the city of Vienna on such and such a date in the first third of the 19th century. Altmayer looked at the seals, looked at me, looked at the names, looked at me again. Meanwhile, I could barely breathe, consumed by nerves. I thought the game was over and I had lost. Suddenly, something appeared to soothe him. 'Everything seems in order,' he said, and I almost wept with joy, but held back. 'Besides,' he added, 'you appear to be an honourable man and will certainly make a better neighbour than Duisdorf. Welcome to Szonden, Redo,' he said cordially; in my anguish, I rose, with the intention of giving him my hand, regretting it immediately when I saw the stunned look on Altmayer's face, who I did not remember having given me permission to stand, and I sat down again. 'As I see you are not familiar with these parts, I must explain some things to you. Utta!' he shouted again, and the servant with brown tangled hair under her bonnet sprung out, as if she were glued to the outside of the door. 'Ask Helmut to wrap up warm and find Hans with my sled and pony.' 'Yes sir,' Utta answered.

'I suppose you have some experience as a farmhand?' *Some.* 'Do you know what a yoke is?' *Yes, the amount of land which a man and a yoke of oxen can plough in a day; I know what that measurement is equivalent to in Austria and France, but not here.* 'An acre, more or less, though here we use the terms horseshoe and half horseshoe, and full or partial sharecropper. Do you know these terms? *No, I don't.* 'You soon will; what you need to know now is that your property amounts to half a horseshoe, more than sufficient for the upkeep of a small household, as yours lamentably is, although I hope not for long.' I chose not to reply. 'You should know that there are two kinds of estate in Prussia: Grundherrschaft and Gutsherrschaft. The latter are more common, both here in the Brandeburg March and in the New March, on the other side of the river. As the name suggests, Gutsherrschaft are connected, or rather were connected, to members of the nobility; I say *were* because successive agrarian reforms, a consequence of the poisonous influence of French ideas, have altered various structures in the kingdom, among them those relating to property. Those incorrigible Jacobins, despite having lost wars and part of their imperial possessions, have won many invisible battles,' Altmayer added, looking at the ceiling, as if talking to himself. 'Anyway, the important thing is – Utta, prepare a bundle!' – 'Yes sir!' was heard beyond the walls of office which I only then noticed was decorated in a martial style – 'that many of the farms surrounding us belong to the lord, Baron Ernst von Geoffman, retired General and Minister of the Prussian Army, decorated with the highest honours after Jena's glorious victory over the French enemy. But the new laws first permitted the handing over of land to tenant farmers, and subsequently the acquisition of rights to small plots; and that scoundrel Duisdorf, whom we shall not miss at all, received, for reasons not worth mentioning, one of the first pieces of free land, although he never managed to cultivate it, and that land is now transferred to you. And so, Redo Hauptshammer, today you are the first free cropper in Szonden and a full citizen of our little town. I shall communicate this to the Prefect and to Berlin, for as you know bureaucracy is the worst of the venereal diseases which the French have been spreading across Europe over recent years, quite something considering the number of horrific plagues they have smuggled in. What will you be cultivating?' The sudden change in register caught me by surprise, and I wriggled out of this fix as best I could: *I will not be able to decide until I've cleared the weeds and examined the soil, sir.* 'A most prudent answer.

You will soon see that around here the crops grown are very traditional. You'll have problems out there, next to the Oder, for when you dig deep you will doubtless find water. You can see the riverbank through this window behind me. Your plot is in that direction.' *Unfortunately, sir, short-sightedness is one of my many limitations. Through that window, except for the ivy sticking out from the frame, I can only make out blurry green and brown patches,* I answered, not lying for once, enviously admiring the eyeglasses resting on Mayor Altmayer's desk. 'Well,' he said somewhat sarcastically, 'your plot is not big enough for that to be a problem.' I didn't know how to respond then. I still don't know now. There was some noise inside the house, and Altmayer stood up. Not knowing if I should get up or not, I leant forward on the chair while still sitting on it, until he granted permission with an unmistakeable look, before then handing me the papers that were my saviour. 'Take your papers and guard them well, although there have been no robberies or any other crimes in Szonden for years. Ever since Duisdorf left, now that I think of it,' and as he laughed loudly I was unsure if I should join in or not; integrating into a different culture is so difficult, even when they do speak the same language. Altmayer congratulated me on my thick beard and told me that another time I should tell him how I kept it in such good condition. We went out to the corridor and then to the main room, where Mrs Ulmer was spying from the corner of her eye while I admired the fine handiwork of her husband's coat and of his military boots. 'This bundle which Utta is handing you contains enough food and drink for a few days. I imagine you and your horse are exhausted.'

Thank you, you're very kind. 'There's no need. I shall also send you some hay and straw so that you and your bay can be comfortable in the cabin. Hans will give you some wood. This is Hans, good morning, Hans.' 'Good morning, Mr Altmayer.' 'This is Redo, your new neighbour. Hans is not a free cropper like you, he's a tenant farmer on a strip of Baron von Geoffman's land just to the south of yours. In a few days I will send a letter informing you of the day and time at which you must pay your respects to Mr von Geoffman.' *Of course, Mayor Altmayer, I'm enormously grateful to you.* I was beginning to breathe. I shook hands with rosy-cheeked Hans, who looked like he'd already had a few beers – which may well have been the case – and we headed out for my new land. I was sorry not to go alone; I would have liked to stop somewhere to scream and rid myself of the nerves that were still seizing me.

I had done it.

The lie, my role, our plan, they had all worked out. Odra would have been proud of me. I had solved the rest of my life, or at least that's what I thought then.

Hans turned out to be a blessing, I don't know how I would have survived without him. Not only did he lend me wood for the fire; to the disapproval of Wiesława, his Lusatian-Polish wife, and to the detriment of his own work, he also helped me turn the big, ramshackle cabin into a habitable dwelling; helped me put away things from my carriage, including the coffin; explained local, regional and national customs and gave me all the support that an owner of cultivable land could hope for from his neighbour. Always attentive and generous, he never demanded any payment in exchange for his help other than my company at the end of the day in Wreech's tavern, because the poor soul was always looking for a companion for drinking, his favourite occupation. At the beginning, out of self-interest, I stayed late, to take advantage of his drink-loosened tongue and gather local information, but, as the days passed, I began to think of poor Wiesława, waiting at home for Hans, sometimes patiently and sometimes not so patiently. So after a couple of white beers – me – and a combination of punch, beer and wine – him – I would walk him home, so that he would arrive there at a reasonable time and in an acceptable condition. Over the years this would endear me to Wiesława, who today loves me like a brother.

Besides, I could not let myself drink too much, and not just for economic reasons. Like everyone, alcohol disinhibits me. And my survival in Szonden now depended on one single requirement: not putting my foot in it, not running my mouth off, not revealing my true origins. Even today, after all these years, I have not once dared to do that. I've never shown my cards. Perhaps I will, maybe no one will mind now. In any case, having recently arrived in Szonden it was imperative I control my language down to the choice and intonation of every last word, as I am doing now as I write this.

To this end Odra and I learnt how not to get drunk, which I will explain at another moment.

I was about to let myself go, just to see *those words*, the words of truth, written down on paper. But I shall wait. After all these years, there's no need to hurry.

4

I have related in part the second day of my arrival in Szonden; if I linger so long on those days it is because they, to a great extent, were the origin of everything that has occurred since, right up to this day, when I need only peer out of the window to witness a dozen feet, the material effects of those strange days.

As I mentioned, I found the Napoleonic twins on the second day, after exhuming the Prussian soldier on the first. On the third morning, as I have also mentioned earlier,[1] beneath copious snowfall and with my mind fixed on Odra, I unearthed four soldiers from vanished Poland before, in desperation, taking the coffin back to the cabin – now the house in which I am writing – so that it would not get cold and so that the wood would not be damaged by the foul weather. Inside the cabin, which back then had two rooms and a cubicle toilet and measured eighteen

---

1 Note that in fact Haupsthammer has *not* already mentioned this discovery. Such memory 'lapses' are constant throughout the manuscript, as much in terms of the facts remembered as with the way those memories are related. In *Diaries of an Inventive Historian,* published posthumously in 1856, Jakob Moltke confirms that, indeed, having recently arrived in Szonden, Haupsthammer discovered four frozen Polish soldiers, in the third of several macabre findings. (Translator's note)

paces north to south and eleven from east to west, the remains of my beloved, my belongings, my straw mattress, my horse and myself all lived together. Hans had helped to rivet the windows and doors to keep out the cold, and we had cleaned out the chimney so that the house could be warmed up and the deep layers of damp disappear from the walls.

On that third day, while I was digging, I remember thinking about moles; I wondered if they could survive in frozen soil or if they had to burrow deep until they found a more favourable stratum to rest in. I remember hearing as a child in Vienna from one of my foolish classmates that moles were completely white with red eyes. I know now that they are brown and that their ocular globes are protected behind a thin layer of vellum, but in my childish imagination, that false description was vividly engraved in my mind, and in my dreams moles are still white creatures looking out into the darkness of the subsoil with bloodshot eyes. I know that this memory came back to me on the third day because, upon seeing a woman whom I shall mention below, I marvelled at the coincidence of having remembered the moles earlier that day.

The morning was clear on the fourth day of my stay in Szonden and I left my hut determined to find a hole in the ground suitable for burying Odra, since stumbling over her coffin every time I moved around my small home provoked deep unease in me. On the one hand, having her remains nearby, as if she were still close, alive in some way, consoled me; on the other hand, something told me that the natural thing was to bury her, bring my state of anaesthetised shock to an end and begin to mourn. In the distance, I could see the three improvised crosses I had placed above the seven bodies, covered once more with earth and blood-stained ice. Revisiting those days now, I understand that they were, without a doubt, the saddest of my life.

I chose another patch of land bordering the path, to limit my cultivable land as little as possible, and began to dig. As my muscles, numbed by the temperature, gradually warmed up, I considered how the water which had been injected into that soil before the arrival of winter was now gradually breaking apart the stones and gravel, causing internal ruptures as it expanded into ice, shattering each particle of soil into smithereens – I am very fond of our German expression, *zu Bruch gehen*; I was amazed that something as fluid and ductile as water could demolish the most solid of rocks. As I stirred, cut, thinned out and distributed the soil with blows of the spade, I thought about the infinitesimal explosions taking place all around me, those miniature grenades silently fragmenting all the space around them, like tiny but efficient mortars, confronting man's determination with the material strength of erosion. 'For that reason' – Hans would later explain from a scientific perspective, something uncommon in a man of his extraction – 'the surface of the globe remains almost identical. If a bird could see us from the heavens and flew over these fields again in 500 years, it would see the exact same image: identical continents and bodies of water, the same river banks, identical mountains and landmasses, despite our pathetic desire to change the planet's forms.'

I was thinking about that storm of minute explosions when I uncovered, in a pocket of congealed blood and soil, the first of eight soldiers dressed in strange uniforms, wearing leather sandals and a kind of skirt instead of trousers, with metal chest guards and short steel swords piled up next to them.

I couldn't believe it. No matter where I dug in that cursed soil I found dead, frozen soldiers, surrounded by their weapons under pools of coagulated blood which announced their presence a few feet further down. What the devil was going on? Was it just a coincidence? Were those bodies the strange fruit of some morbid mania? Had Duisdorf been a collector of dead soldiers? Was this Duisdorf's reason for abandoning Szonden and ridding himself of his property? Was that strip of farmland a joke, a curse, was it born from a desire to have an illicit burial ground for non-Christians? But the old Poles were probably Catholics, and the Prussian soldier found on the first day would surely have been faithful to Luther's doctrine, like most of the inhabitants of Oderbruch and the Brandeburg March.

I felt so lost that I went to notify Hans, who scratched his head and told me that many years earlier he had uncovered a skeleton while digging in his field to build a well; the remains seemed to have been buried for decades, perhaps the result of an ancient war or battle, or some other natural circumstance. 'You may not be aware that some of these fields are the fruit of the drainage and fertilization project which the great king Frederick William II carried out in this region.' Perhaps Hans did not express himself thus, but I like to remember or imagine him talking like that, besides, I'm no journalist, I have no duty to tell the truth. 'In past times,' Hans continued, 'the banks of the Oder were uncultivable swamps, difficult to traverse and dangerous for men and beasts. But the land our plots are on is of a very high quality, partly because of the rain and partly because of the clay. There are few rocks under the soil, which makes them ideal for growing. Or burying. Or fighting. Jakob, the historian, will know all about that. Have you spoken to him yet?' *No, I don't know him.* 'You'll certainly find him at Wreech's tavern this evening. He knows almost everything, and will tell you exactly who those warriors are. I fear you will also have to bring Mayor Altmayer and the school headteacher up to speed.' *Why the headteacher?* 'Because he's also our church pastor. In small towns the two duties are always taken by the same person.' *Ah.* 'You'll soon be familiar with our customs.' *Yes. Thank you for the explanation, Hans, now I know what to do, but... should I leave the bodies where they are?* 'I would keep them there until Altmayer decides what to do.' *Altmayer? But they're in my field, shouldn't I decide?* 'I don't know the laws regarding free land. On my land, I wouldn't touch a thing without first informing Baron Geoffmann.' *I hope no more remains appear, I need to start planting straight away.* 'What are you going to plant?' *Sugar beet. It's the only thing that can prosper in this frozen soil, provided it's turned and fertilised.* 'Good choice. No one plants beet here, we prefer to go for the safe choices: potatoes, hops, vegetables, wheat.' *All the more reason not to create a surplus: I can't show up in the town and offer something you have all been producing for years.* 'That's sensible.' *Besides that, I must dedicate a small portion of the land to my own survival.* 'Of course, we all do that. I think things will go well for you, Redo, you know what you want. The beet leaves can also be used to feed your animals; I recommend you cut the leaves yourself by hand, so that the beasts don't damage the plants when they eat them.' *Thank you, Hans, I don't know what I would have done without your help. I'll come and find you at nightfall to offer you a warm beer.* 'Facing a long day of work is easier after hearing those words. Until then,' he said, taking his leave with a smile.

And there I remained, wringing my hands, my new burial pit half uncovered.

After dedicating the rest of the day to weeding the field and clearing the scrub, I went early to the tavern early, when darkness fell, to see if I could find this historian, Jakob. By chance, Jakob had also decided to come to the pub to meet the strange foreigner who had just settled in the town. Rumours were beginning to spread about me, the new arrival, which was somewhat predictable given the lack of gossip sources in the small town, the previous owner's bad reputation and the fact that I was one of the first people in the Oderbruch, and the first in Szonden, to obtain a liberated property, in a region generally subject to the whims of Baron Ernest von Geoffman, cousin of one of the prince-electors and a former general and minister of the armed forces, as I was constantly being reminded. In addition, his portrait presided, along with the royal effigy, over the tavern owned by Wreech, whose fierce face, framed by a copious blond mane, moved inside that room like a caged lion, although now that I think of it I have never seen a lion and only know them from descriptions and engravings in books. This goes for almost everything, as I have seen little of the world and plenty of paper.

The tavern was noticeably big, with adjoining tables made from walnut wood and long benches where the parishioners sat down to chat, play cards or sing drunkenly, depending on the hour of the day or the day of the week. I sat down in a corner and took two fistfuls of seeds from my pockets to do my accounts with. I could write a little by then,[2] but I preferred not to reveal either my skills or my defects yet, except for the obvious one, my short sight, until I had a better idea of my new countrymen. Wreech approached me, extending his hand as he examined me in detail. 'You're Redo, aren't you? I've seen you here a few times, although my wife has always served you. Welcome to my inn, I'm Wreech and the beer I'm serving you now is the first and last that you will drink here free of charge.' He smiled faintly and I shook his hand as firmly as I could and smiled back. Then he went back to his work, and no sooner had he turned away than he once more adopted that severe expression men and women over fifty have when life has not worked out as they had expected, that is, the majority of people on the globe. My face displays less tension because, given the place and conditions in which my birth, childhood and youth transpired, I have never been in a position to expect anything at all from life.

---

2 We will recall that Redo had told Mayor Altmayer, in the conversation reproduced some pages back, that he could hardly read at all. (Translator's note)

I took out the reddish seeds and did some sums, making a pile representing all my savings and considering what to do with them. A small amount of seeds were gathered to one side, indicating that they would be reserved for restoring the cabin and gradually turning it into a house, wall by wall and tile by tile; it would not be a tough job since I had learnt that trade from my uncle Sigfredo over a few summers at his country house in Linz. Bricklaying is a skill that does not demonstrate its incredible utility until you need it. Another more numerous group of seeds remained in the middle of the table. It was the most decisive, and was bovine in form, sometimes an ox and other times a cow. Those seeds did not represent enough money to acquire both animals. Either I bought an ox to help me plough or made do with a cow to guarantee myself fresh milk, yoghurts, cheeses and eventual calves. With the ox the work in the fields would be faster, less arduous and extremely productive: its strength would permit me to use a big plough to aerate and fertilise the earth more efficiently. But then I would have to buy milk and other foods every day, which meant that if the harvest went badly I would have nothing to substitute it until the following season. If I opted for the cow I could only use a tiny plough, pulled by the horse. I took a sip from my beer, savouring it; they obviously knew how to make it in this region. I organised other small heaps of grain on the table, representing smaller investments in hens, tools, goods for the home and a thermometer and scales, which Hans had told me would be indispensable for certain tasks such as making cheeses and sweets.

The arrival of two men at the tavern interrupted the course of my musings. They both removed their hats as they entered and, upon seeing me, walking straight in my direction. They wore thick, good quality bearskin jackets, and the bigger man had a marten skin draped over his shoulders. This man introduced himself as vice-rector Stein and quickly apologised since in he would have to depart for Lebus in a few minutes on an assignment from the Archbishopric. He promised to come and visit me later and bade me a polite farewell. The other man, shorter yet more robust, was dressed in a way that was both discreet and elegant: his soft, fine rentier's hands and his intelligent expression made me suspect that I was looking at the historian Jakob Moltke, a suspicion he immediately confirmed. It's strange to go back to the moment at which two people who are still unaware that they will forge a great friendship meet; there is no sign announcing it, nor signals in the air, yet somehow these people feel comfortable from the very start, as if they were not meeting for the first time but merely being reunited after a brief separation.

I gathered up the seeds to clear a space on the table, upon seeing that Wreech was walking over with a large jug of dark beer, which Jakob received with a nod and which he had not even needed to order. 'I had been told that you were an evasive, strange man, but you seem quite normal; only your complexion gives away the fact that you are a foreigner, somewhat thinner than is usual in this region of hardy peasants and gentlemen with experience in battle and the physical exercise of the military encampments.' *That makes sense, I've only been dedicated myself to agricultural labour for a few months,* I answered, once again fully self-conscious of my language and beginning to carefully measure the quantity of beer drunk and the rhythm of its consumption, since I could not forget the part that I would always have to act out. 'Ah, that explains things. In no time at all you'll be as muscly as any of our lads,' Jakob said, smiling. *I've heard that you are a historian,* I mentioned as I clinked my mug against his. 'Yes, I devote my time to talking about the past as if it were a close relative. My real family, who benefit from a distant connection to the Hohenzolern, has possessions in the New March and in the Königsberg region, where Kant was from. Do you know Kant? You will soon, or at least, you will hear about him soon. From me, most likely.' He smiled and I did so too simultaneously, like a mirror. I also drank beer whenever he did, because people adore physical symmetries and coincidences, and creating them is the most direct route to successful seduction and the earning of trust: my mother taught me that, part of the store of knowledge handed down by an old prostitute so that I could manage the brothel's finances, since it was highly improbable that I could become a *Madame* when she retired. 'If you focus the conversation on what you both have in common, or if you force or invent coincidences regarding your tastes, you can make a lot of headway,' Andrea would tell us on the worn armchairs in the green room, during quiet periods. I managed to come back from those mental scenes in Vienna before Jakob could think that I was distracted or that he was boring me. For the moment, his philosophical references did not allow me to establish any association at all, so I adopted the second infallible technique

38

for gaining someone else's sympathy: listening attentively to the other person's monologue, a trick which works especially well with Narcissus-like temperaments such as that of my dear Jakob, whom I miss so much now in these dull, placid years. 'My ancestors' wealth has afforded my brothers and I the chance to live at ease, without having to depend on the land. Numerous landlords and tenant farmers work on our land and we give them some of the profits. With an annual income of thousands of talers I have more than enough to live here' – melancholically, I weighed up what I could do if I had thousands of talers every year; now, happily, I do – 'I chose Szonden because of its tranquillity and the beauty of the river. There is a beautiful view over the river bank in the part where your farm is situated.' *I share your appreciation. I don't know how I will ever work with so much beauty before me.* 'I sometimes think that when I walk through the town, which is why I usually stay in my house in the mornings, so as not to be distracted from my studies. Besides the natural gifts of the landscape, I'm often distracted by another kind of beauty, that of the land's inhabitants. Have you glimpsed Johanna, Mr von Geoffman's daughter, or the miller, Ingeborg? Good God, what fine women, and I a bachelor! It's lucky I have my faithful lover, History, to remind me that all endeavours are futile and all passions transitory.' *Unfortunately, as a widower I couldn't agree more.* I took advantage of the sympathy I saw in his face to make my petition. *Hans mentioned that you could help me figure out some symbols I found in my plot.* 'What kind of symbols? Lusatian, Saxon, Viking runes? Numerous cultures have left their mark here.' *It's complicated, it would be better if you saw it with your own eyes, if it's not too much bother. I wouldn't ask if it wasn't important.* 'That's no problem, tomorrow I will come by at the first hour of the afternoon, if that suits you.'

Hans entered the tavern, his face red from the cold, took off his felt cap and greeted me when he saw me with the historian, smiling as if to say: 'Hello, Redo, I note that you are in a conclave and must keep your attention on conversation, whereas I have come here not to sustain my attention but to let it fade; so, if you don't mind, I'll head to the back to play *Dreikart* and drink beer with the peasants, while you continue to rub shoulders with more prominent members of local society'; for my part, I smiled and lifted my mug in his direction by way of greeting and assent, certain that Hans would walk through that door again in a couple of hours as red as when he entered, though not from the cold.

Jakob congratulated me on the care I took to look after my copious beard, and after a bit of small talk, broached the topic: 'What are you going to sow on your plot, Redo?' I was beginning to be aware of the extent to which, in small towns and perhaps everywhere else, you are what you cultivate. I took a red beet seed from the pocket of my only clean jacket and placed it in his hand. 'I'm no expert in these matters. To my eyes it could be hop, canary seed, pepper, any herb or spice.' *I'm delighted to see that there is something you don't know.* 'What I don't know defines me, and many things define me.' I liked that answer, I could greatly identify with it. I thought, as he sipped his beer and I explained a few things about beet and sugar, that Jakob Moltke, educated but not

40

overbearing, was the kind of man I would like to have as a friend.

I left the pub with a stabbing pain in my chest, missing Odra dreadfully. I would have liked to tell her about all I had experienced on that pleasant afternoon, or the day before, the good and the bad, but I couldn't tell her anything, couldn't rest my head on her chest, couldn't kiss her, couldn't make new plans or share my joy that things were going according to our original plans. During the bittersweet return home I bumped into an unsettling figure; a small, thin woman, wrapped in a covering of skin or fabric I couldn't recognise but which resembled ermine. Her own skin was disconcertingly white, beyond mere paleness and closer to transparency. Her hair was long and white, not grey but *white*, and it poured down smoothly from her uncovered head. As we passed one another I could see that her irises were a dark shade of red, and I stammered a greeting as she pierced me with her fiery look. She did not respond and kept walking uphill towards the town centre. I realised that I had seen an albino; I had heard talk of albinos in Vienna but never seen one. I reached my land and in the weak moonlight I could just make out the Prussian's tomb and the four pits; I thought about Odra's coffin, waiting inside for me, and a shiver went down my spine as I considered that I was about to sleep surrounded by dead bodies.

The following morning was even colder, but the sky was clear at least. In my bed, disheartened and terribly sad, for I could see my beloved's funerary box, I considered bringing the buried corpses to the surface, so that Jakob could see them in the afternoon, but then I dismissed the idea, since it would be easy to uncover them by tossing the soil; at least while covered no scavenger bird, insect or rodent could come close. Although the soldiers were completely frozen and it would be difficult to damage them, I preferred to keep any animals at bay out of respect. I walked across the entire plot to slowly take in the extent of my property: a narrow strip of land slightly elevated where it backed onto the river, creating a sort of plateau; I examined the frozen soil, intending to take definitive decisions, since I had to settle now on a cow or an ox and begin work. The continual snowfall guaranteed sufficient water for the planted seeds to grow, but of course it was necessary to sow them. I also had to clear the scrub and choose which part of the farm to use as an allotment, depending on the kind of soil, although it all seemed favourable. I crouched down and touched the earth. It was frozen, yes, but on previous days, when I touched the corpses, I got the impression that they were more frozen than the soil surrounding them. They felt like pure ice and their temperature was rather lower than that of the clumps of earth I now held in my hand. I got up, shaking my hands, and felt a presence behind me. I turned around and there, indeed, was a lackey in gleaming footwear, his hands behind his back. This is one of the problems with being short-sighted: by the time you see others they have already been observing you for some time. His fine winter boots were covered in mud from my field. 'Redo Haupsthammer?' *Yes.* 'I come on behalf of Mr Ernest von Geoffman. He wants to see you.' *Ah yes,*

Mayor Altmayer mentioned. When does he want me to visit? 'Now is a good time.' *Now? It's seven in the morning.* The servant said nothing, as if he was well aware that it was seven in the morning and that, despite this, he had been at work for some time. *Of course,* I said gladly, hiding my irritation. A gleaming, spotless carriage awaited us. Just as I was about to get inside, the servant reprimanded me: 'Excuse me, that's where gentlemen go. You come up here with me,' and he pointed to a place beside him in the driver's seat. We travelled in silence through the icy air to the Lord of Szonden's ample residence; for a long stretch the Oder flowed peacefully, its surface frozen on the edges while the wide central torrent resisted the ice. The view, as far as I could appreciate it, was magnificent, full of enormous trees extending their branches towards the wavering morning light.

The Lord of Szonden's estate was bigger than some of the towns I had seen on my journey to the Oderbruch. It was sumptuous in appearance, although a careful observer, which I am if I can get close enough, could detect some signs of decay in the mansion: little cracks, unrepaired masonry, chipped floorboards, damp patches, bare walls just out of sight, tiles colonised by weeds. This is the only advantage of having experienced so much decay, you detect it instantly wherever you go. I couldn't see the lesser details until I was almost entering the building, since from afar I couldn't make out much more than an immense white continuum with vertical or diagonal wooden tiles. The coachman made me wait at the door while far off I watched some hens scuttling away, pursued by two small figures, impossible to say from that distance if they were boys or girls. Then a female servant, who stood still for a second, gazing at my beard – it's not uncommon for people, after drinking a few beers, to ask permission to touch and caress it – allowed me in and made me stand waiting next to the staircase. I took advantage of this to admire what looked like a portrait of the lady of the house: a splendid woman, resplendent with jewels and character. After some time, an aide in livery came down the staircase and ordered me to come up, pointing to a discreet stool on the luxurious upper floor where I was to sit and wait for the lord to call me in. I was there for no less than twenty minutes, surrounded by an absolute silence broken only by a female voice singing fragments of a French song from somewhere in the house. I remembered that the use of French is habitual among German and Russian aristocrats, and for that reason I forced myself to add to the list of my obligations that of acting as if I had no knowledge whatsoever of the language. As I had time to think, I considered this further: *you neither know nor don't know French, you say nothing on the subject; if the baron discovers after the fact that you do speak French he will distrust you, and justifiably so. Say nothing either way.* I am always grateful to that tiny and elusive person hidden deep inside me, who gives me sound advice whenever I have the time to go down to my catacombs and find her among all that inner noise. I call her Regina, because that was my grandmother's name; she had abundant common sense, according to my mother, I never knew her. Regina is that tiny part of me which possesses reason, and because of that I almost never find her. Her voice is always drowned out by the braggart Helmut,

44

uncaring Peter, and various other pig-headed, deleterious inner demons who get carried away by the slightest impulse. 'Come in, Lord von Geoffman is waiting for you. Remember that you are in the company of a member of the nobility and a war hero.' *I know how to behave, thank you. In Vienna I dealt with many gentlemen and ministers, though it may not appear so.* 'It doesn't.' *I wish you a good day of labour and servitude, I'll think of you in a few hours when I find myself once more in my liberated field, with no master or lord.* I like to light up the faces of imbeciles with rage and had to suppress my smile as I entered the spacious library of Lord Ernest von Geoffman, who received me seated, reading. He looked up at me over his gold-rimmed glasses. 'My word, we have before us the first free landowner in Szonden,' he said, and I couldn't tell if he was being sarcastic or corroborating a fact. 'Your name is Redo Haus...' *Hauptshammer.* 'Hauptshammer, yes, we should be more familiar with Austrian surnames, since we are now allies since the peace treaty signed in Vienna, although unfortunately one can't get on with such big neighbours for too long. In the book I have just been reading it says: "try above all to expel civil conflict, which is enmity", although I'm not sure we will achieve that.' *Europe isn't big enough for so many kings,* I replied. Lord von Geoffman looked at me, not quite clear if he was in the presence of a wise man or a perfect idiot. I realised that I might have thrown down a very large gauntlet and lowered the tension. *I hope I have not seemed impertinent, I was only repeating a saying I heard some years ago in Vienna. I imagine there are people there who think the same as your grace. In any case, I no longer consider myself Austrian but an adoptive son of Szonden, if I may be so bold, like a newborn waiting to be accepted by his new community.* I intentionally avoided the word *family*. The baron appeared to relax: 'There is no doubt that will be the case, here we have nothing against those who come and bring work and wealth to the town. I have been told you were recently widowed.' *Yes. It has not been six days since I lost my wife in Mainz. I have not accepted the loss yet; in fact, I have not even been able to bury her...* Just at that moment a door that had been hidden in the back wall opened abruptly, and through it appeared a brown-haired angel of some eighteen years whose excessive beauty I could not take in at that distance, dressed in tight clothing which revealed most desirable shapes. I, however, contemplated her like someone looking at a beautiful painting, in the same way that I had admired her mother depicted in oil paint, because my heart and my body were still anaesthetised to all stimuli. 'Forgive me for interrupting, father, I have something to show you.' 'I'll come shortly, Johanna, when I'm finished with this man.' The girl looked at me with curiosity, no doubt because I had not immediately surrendered before her exceptional charms, as all men, everywhere, every day, surely did in her presence. She closed the door. 'What will you grow, Redo?' I felt the blow: the powerful lord did not even remember what I carried with me at every moment: Odra, whose passing I was talking about before the interruption. I felt out of place, worn out. Alone. *Well... my intention is not to inconvenience anyone, and it would not be wise on my part to arrive as a foreigner in a new place and compete with established producers. That's why I've thought about a crop which, as far as I know, you will know better than me, is*

46

not grown in Szonden: sugar beet. 'Beet,' he said, pensively, before adding, 'Interesting. But what do you aim to do with it once it's been gathered?' *Take it to Magdeburg, the refinery there will buy it from me. It's only a day and a half's journey.* 'The Coqui processor... Good thinking.' The baron looked at me with a certain curiosity. 'You're different, you don't seem like a peasant.' *I've only been one for a short time. In Vienna I managed accounts for a business.* 'Interesting. Why did you leave?' Anyone else would have added, 'May I ask', or, 'if you don't mind', but I was in the presence of the man who had been, and in some ways still was, the Lord of Szonden. *I had the opportunity to stop working for others and do it for myself.* 'Ah, I see. You're not a peasant, of course, I forgot. You are now a *proprietor*. You want to make money because you believe you know how to.' I admit this surprised me. I realised the baron was no fool. I restricted myself to giving him an intelligent look, now that I knew he could recognise intelligence in others. 'All right, Redo. A most fruitful conversation. Your accounting knowledge may come in helpful, or rather, useful at some moment.' *Feel free to bring up anything, sir.* I don't know if Geoffmann was expecting me to say 'at your service' or something similar, but I wanted to make it clear from the beginning that the possibility of my help – and the extra work would be very welcome – would have a price. Social convention meant I had to show the baron respect, but it was not obligatory to pay homage. 'I will accompany you downstairs, but first I'm going to see what my daughter wants. Wait here, please.' The 'please' which the noble uttered before going through the door from which his heiress had appeared made me hope for a reasonable future deal. When I was left alone I couldn't avoid staring at the glasses on the table. They were of superlative quality. I had never used glasses, I had always thought I could see enough, if not as much as my congeners, and there was never enough money in Vienna to pay for what my mother would have considered a luxury. In an inexplicably daring act, since I am normally respectful with others' belongings, I walked over to Baron von Geoffman's desk, took his glasses and put them on before the window.

After an instant's hesitation, my eyes adjusted and discovered the trees in the landscape, the branches in the trees, the green leaves swaying on the branches. All of them. One by one. I saw each blade of grass. I saw the ripples on the surface of the Oder. I saw for the first time that there are different tones in the shadows the sun casts over objects. I saw distant, snow-capped mountains, which I had not seen before. I saw that the most distant ones seemed to be veiled in fog, while the nearest ones did not. I saw dozens of birds flying in the distance. I discovered that the clouds are not indistinct blotches in the sky; they have bulbs, shapes, patterns, curves, folds.

On the brink of tears, I left the baron's glasses, with which I had perceived reality in all its perfection, on the table.

5

I refused the coach I was offered because I wanted time to think on the walk back. I concluded that although practical matters had thus far prospered reasonably well – in the aftermath of Odra's death I preferred not to think about other things, since inside I was like a barren desert – such advances were down to courage rather than prudence. The baron glimpsed in me the same personal project that Odra and I had mapped out. Now was not the moment to back down; something told me that even if the harvest was poor, the hospitality I had encountered in the town would keep me from dying of hunger. Despite being a foreigner and a newcomer, I had encountered nothing but kindness there. Yes, my mind was made up. I would buy the ox. I had some savings hidden in a secret corner of my carriage, the fruits of our sacrifices in Vienna and France, and a new possibility was emerging on the horizon: using my accounting skills. It was a profession I knew well, I thought as I walked along the river, work suited for night-time, when no other productive labour can be done. Because I lived alone and had not the slightest intention of seeking company, since for several reasons there would never be any other woman but Odra, I had ample time from which to extract profit. I understood that true freedom, the kind Jakob enjoyed, arose from the complete satisfaction of all primary needs. That is, when the margin of risk only affects less important aspects of life, not the principal ones: subsistence, health and a small estate that allows you to face the future with confidence. I was fully aware that I was a long way off such a status; but I also knew that the most direct path to tranquillity would require several years of supreme effort.

Thinking about Jakob reminded me of part of the previous night's conversation. His various concerns, so different from those which had occupied and preoccupied me thus far, attracted me like a magnet. As I walked by the Oder, I reconstructed his monologue: 'I'm helping Mährlen, the historian, with a decisive work, *Die Geschichte unerer Tage*. He knows how interested I am in making a history of the present, starting from the *idea* of the present, focussing on the past not as a point of arrival but of departure.' I nodded, as if I knew what he was talking about, to make him feel good. 'Do you know that, in the last thirty years, no less than forty expressions have come into our language which allude to the current moment, the present tense? Do you not find this revealing of the fact that we now find ourselves before a moment of wider change, one in which we redefine our idea of ourselves.' *My mother used to say that she could detect how distressed the people she worked with were from the number of allusions, veiled or explicit, that they made to their immediate circumstances.* 'Exactly! Wider trends end up reverberating in people's language.' That concerned me: such unconscious reverberation was just what I had to avoid at all costs to remain safe in Szonden. 'If you don't mind my asking, Redo, what was your mother's work?' I had never expected such a question, and improvised an answer as we walked into the tavern. *She... my mother provided services for Viennese professionals, she was a sort of saleswoman: sedatives, lenitives, tranquilisers, emollients, that sort of thing. You cannot imagine how many people in big cities require rapid relief from tension. The best doctors and pharmacists frequently depended on her services. And she also provided instant tranquillity to judges, generals, ministers, et cetera. Because such important figures must, for urgent reasons of state, not show their anxieties and worries in public...* 'Naturally.' *Their commercial relationships with my mother were kept strictly secret, but the fact that her work took place behind the scenes did not mean it was any less transcendental for the King of Austria's health, and it remained so until his death three years ago.* 'I am very sorry.' *Thank you, Mr Moltke.* 'Just Jakob, please.' *Thank you, Jakob. In any case, the important women in my life are dead and I have no close family left. I'm alone in the world,* I added, controlling my emotions and the tone in which I enunciated them as much as I could. I sipped my beer to avoid an uncomfortable moment. There was no room for error, ever; I had to remain forever alert while communicating, and I remain on guard now, though there may no longer be any need for it. That's something I've been mulling over recently. Perhaps it's not mere chance that this unease coincides with a pressing need to put my memories down in writing. Jakob proposed a toast: 'May our lives be fruitful and may we see better years.' He confessed that he too was alone in the world but that he had got used to it, before rapidly changing the subject, to ward off the ghosts.

When I returned from the baron's estate, my decision to buy the ox already set in stone, instead of going to my land I headed straight to see Hans, who at this early hour was already sweating with the effort of pulling the yoke. I asked him where in town I could acquire an ox, hens, a plough and the other goods and tools I needed to begin work. Hans was delighted by my decision and offered me all his support, telling me with touching tranquillity what I had known ever since I first looked him in the eye: that as long as he was living there and in good health I would always have food on my table. And that in the unlikely case everything went wrong for me, we would join the two fields and I would divide the work with him. I was close to tears. If hugs had not been completely prohibited I would have hugged him right there, but I controlled myself and shook his hand firmly, thanking him for his kind words from the bottom of my heart. 'Although she does not know you yet, Wiesława already holds you in affection; she says that since your arrival, I come home earlier and in a better state,' he joked. 'So I think she'd happily look after you too, if necessary.'

I dedicated the rest of the day to my purchases and labour, which allowed me to get to know more people in Szonden; perhaps I will return to some of them later, but for now it's enough to say that I felt very welcome. I was the novelty in a place with little news and was being constantly questioned, an ideal situation for refreshing, weaving and fine tuning my lies. At the first hour of the afternoon I returned to my field to await Jakob, with whom I had arranged to consult on the question of the frozen bodies. To my surprise, the historian, and my future friend, was already there, crouching down before one of the crosses, surprise written on his face. Without looking up, for I imagine he had already seen me some time ago, he said: 'You're going to have to let Mayor Altmayer and the vice-rector know about this.' *Yes, Hans said the same thing.* 'But... have you opened the tombs? Did you find the field like this or did you find a corpse in each place as you were digging?' *I wish it were only one corpse per cross, Jakob. Beneath that one lies a Prussian soldier, between that one there, two grenadiers from Napoleon's army; in the furthest one, four more soldiers, who Hans thinks are Polish. And now I want to show you what lies beneath this one, the strangest thing of all.'* 'What you have just told me is pretty strange already.' *One moment.* I ran into the cabin to get the spade and to remove my thick coat. Without uttering a word, I came back and started digging; as I suspected, the soil was easier to move once it had been stirred. In just a few minutes I started to uncover the first of the exotic, skirt-clad warriors I had found. As I went about uncovering the others, Jakob carefully lowered himself into the hole and examined the first body. 'It's completely frozen, how is that possible? It's certainly very cold, but not even the Oder is completely frozen. You only need to touch this soil to see that its temperature is several degrees higher than that of the corpse.' *Yes,* I sighed, panting as I continued to dig up earth from the pit. 'These soldiers... It's impossible,' he muttered. 'Impossible.' His faced revealed utter bewilderment. He was about to lift his hands to his head, but just before doing it he realised they were covered in earth and placed them back down on his waist. This amused me, since I was already up to my knees in mud. We both got out of the enormous hole and looked down from the edge. Eight warriors, all very young, three of them bearded, all more or less the same height and perfectly conserved from being completely frozen. 'Redo, I don't know what to tell you. If they weren't as cold as icicles and thus dead, I'd say this must be a joke. But it's not funny at all. These poor boys' uniforms are Roman, surely belonging to the XIX Legion that lost the battle during the massacre of Teotoburg in the year 9. These soldiers must have formed a *contubernium,* which met its death here for some reason. But that's insanity, for how could they still be unscathed, as if recently dead, these bodies which must have lived and died nineteen centuries ago. I've heard that in some glaciers...' he said softly to himself, as if seeking an explanation, and stroking his chin, so deep in concentration that he forgot about the mud. 'No, it makes no sense. Are all the other bodies the same?' *Yes, all the same. Frozen, perfectly conserved. And they stay frozen even after exposure to the sun and air.* 'That's impossible.' *You've used that word several times, and so have I over the last few days. Perhaps we need to find another. Because there they are, looking at us.* Indeed, four or five of the soldiers had their eyes open and seemed to be looking at us. *So fresh.* Jakob could not help smiling. 'Don't be disrespectful, Redo.' *I'm sorry, but there comes a point when I can't take this seriously, if only to conserve my sanity. Every time I dig into this earth, corpses appear. Double the number each time, to be precise.* 'What? I don't understand.' *You heard me. On the first day I found one soldier; the second, two, the third, four, and the fourth, yesterday, I found these eight bodies.* 'In that order?' *Yes, it's not easy to forget.* 'But... It must be a coincidence, that you uncovered them in that order.' *I believe in coincidences, Jakob, until they occur four times consecutively.* The historian looked at the contubernium, lost for words. *Let's put it to the test, I'll dig somewhere else and sixteen bodies will appear...* 'Listen, Redo, you can't bury your wife here, you must do it in the burial ground next to the church.' *Odra wasn't baptised,* I told him, looking him in the eye. He nodded. 'In that case, this is the place for her.' *I'll try that corner.*

We walked over to the edge of the opposite boundary and I began digging into the earth; as it was frozen and intact, each incision required great effort. After what seemed like an eternity I found coagulated blood, four feet deep, the now familiar foreshadowing of what was waiting further down. I hit the first body at three thirty in the afternoon, the seventh at five – Jakob offered to take turns with the spade but I refused outright, because he was older than me and dressed in fine clothes – and found body number 16 long after sunset. During that time I took several pauses, naturally, to rest and to greet the numerous people who came over to contemplate this arduous spectacle: Mayor Altmayer, who had come to look for Jakob, Hans, vice-rector Stein – who was only there for a moment, apologising because he had to go to Reitwein on business but adding that he would be back within a few days to introduce himself properly – one of Altmayer's officials, a sullen redhead called Finkhölmer, and a couple of parishioners who happened to walk past. By dinnertime, my land was a beehive of people coming in and out of the two open pits to see, by the light of a pair of improvised torches and a hand lamp, and touch the corpses, whose frozen state they thought impossible until they came up close and felt them with their own hands. The fire was reflected in the thin ice and the flames could be seen in the stunned eyes of all present. Some looked at me with solidarity, imagining the drama this situation would entail for me. At one moment I asked Altmayer what was to be done, because I couldn't leave those bodies there. 'Well, they can't be buried in the usual places when we're not certain of their identities or even if they've been baptised.' *What about burying them in some communal land?* Jakob and Altmayer looked at each other and Altmayer said what anyone who hadn't the faintest idea what to do would say: 'I must discuss it with the Prefect. I will also mention it to Mr von Geoffman, since after all the dead are soldiers. The first one you found may even have fought under his command.' *And what am I to do in the meantime? I have to sow, my ox and equipment arrive tomorrow.* Altmayer shrugged his shoulders. He didn't know what to say but couldn't acknowledge it in public. I suggested some possibilities. *Will you give me permission to pile them up by the path? They won't thaw.* 'That seems disrespectful to me.' *Hmmm, let's see... can I at least bury all of them together in one corner?* 'Covered in soil?' *Yes, I could cover them. It will be hellish work, but I will cover them.* Hans offered his help, and both my outer and inner voices thanked him for this. Altmayer added: 'You must rest a little, Redo. It's most admirable that you have done all this work alone in a single afternoon, given your lack of bulk.' *Thank you for your understanding, mayor.* What's certain is that I had never felt exhaustion – not just in the physical sense – like that which took hold in that instant. I said

goodbye to all my neighbours with the greatest of consid-
eration, thanking them for their support. My land looked
like a battlefield. I entered the house, stoked the fire, gave
the horse some straw and oats and kissed Odra's coffin,
before falling like a dead man onto the mattress. Those
were the facts. But the most important thing was a conversation between Jakob and Altmayer, which I shall try
to reconstruct.

Andrea Böhm always boasts of having been born at the
only time a woman reigned over one of Europe's most
powerful territories. She is proud to have lived her earli-
est years when the nation was ruled by Maria Theresa I,
then archduchess and queen of Austria, Hungary, Croatia
and Bohemia, not to mention duchess of Mantua, Milan,
Galicia, Lodomeria, Parma and the Austrian Low Countries and also, after her marriage, duchess of Lorrain and
Tuscany and Empress Consort of the Holy Roman Empire. When Andrea was born, Vienna was a beautiful,
prosperous metropolis of 215,000 people, the develop-
ment of which the queen contributed to. 'It's wonderful
to have seen all that power in the hands of a woman with
so much personality,' she often tells us, doubtless so that
we always give her the same answer: 'You have power
and personality too, mother,' or, 'you're our Maria Theresa
I,' we tell her, and she laughs, downplaying it with a hand
gesture. 'Over these months you must learn all the most
important things,' she tells us, now serious. 'I will be gone
soon and this house must keep going.' We tell her that her
noble leadership has been the best possible lesson and
that our years alongside her have been the best school.

She raises an eyebrow as she looks at us, graciously scolding us for our flattery. We only want her to be content until the end, to feel cherished and important until the last moment. What can be bad about that? Sometimes she sits down sullenly in a corner, adjusting her bodice, looking discreetly out the window after opening the net curtains, yellowed with time and tobacco. She can't go out on the streets like before, awakening the admiration of men and women with her graceful movements. I wish I had inherited some of her physical virtues, but of all the gifts she gave me, the physical do not number among them. I'm big and clumsy. I have her aptitude for control, the girls tell me, but only that. Her iron will. That's why I have taken refuge in other things. Sometimes she looks at us, when Odra and I are alone with her, and says: 'I know what's happening. I don't approve of your relationship but then who am I, a brothel keeper, to give lessons in decency.' And we laughed. Andrea Böhm is my mother. And Böhm is my real name. Hauptshammer isn't my surname but the one Odra and I chose to put some distance between my past and my person. In the same way, we thought Redo would be a plausible name for me. It's difficult to get used to a name that isn't yours, but, mother says, 'you'll get used to it when you've been called it for as long as you were called the first one.' I hope she's right. In any case, when you don't know who your father is surnames don't matter much, as there's no way of symbolically linking it with your progenitor. Andrea believes my father was a soldier she was involved with, one of several, at the end of the century. *Why do you think it was him?* 'I don't know. When we were finished I felt like I had been impregnated.' We laughed. *That's impossible.* 'I know,' she replies, enigmatic and serious. When I see a high-ranking military officer of a certain age effusively saluting Andrea I can't help thinking he might be my father. I miss Andrea. I miss Odra. I long for them both. Life in Vienna back then was terrible for everyone, especially for Odra; but now, forgive me, my beloved, I remember it as a happy time, because you were both alive.

I was going to relate the conversation between Jakob and Altmayer on the day the sixteen bodies were exhumed but I have digressed a little. Don't hold it against me, blame a novice narrator's inexperience. I get distracted by phrases and memories, and forget that a long text, as Jakob used to tell me, must have a structure, like a building.

'I don't recognise these uniforms, I've never seen them before. Do you have any idea, Moltke, which army they belong to?' By torchlight, Jakob's wavering figure seemed dark and enormous, like the history of the world. 'Mayor, I confess, this affair has completely blindsided me. In these lands and beyond, in the territory between Berlin and Kostrzyn, battles have been fought from antiquity to the present day, between Bohemians from Hus, ancient Ugro-Finns, Pomeranians, Austrians, Russians, Roman legions, soldiers from extinct Poland, Cossacks, the French, Saxons, Suevian Semnones, Swedes (and before them the Scandinavian *Soe Kongar* and Vikings, as unpredictable as a storm), a battalion of Irishmen under the command of Duke Walter de Butler, Wends, Spaniards following the orders of the Duke of Marradas, Ascanian Slavs, three generations of Prussians and even Kalmyks from distant

Mongolia. I am almost certain that these sophisticated uniforms do not belong to any of those armies.' 'Then which army do they belong to?' 'I don't know, I expect our forces have no contact with them. They carry very sophisticated pistols, small and easy to handle, made using technology far superior to ours. Their uniforms are of unknown tailoring and appear to be perfect. Of the symbols they bear I only recognise a variation on an old meso-oriental cross with bent arms. I don't know what it means, I'll have to look at my books on ancient symbology. Believe me when I say I am utterly lost. And concerned.' *Why?* I asked, curious. 'Because the existence of a modern, well-equipped army of which we are completely unaware is not desirable,' Baron Geoffman pronounced from behind me. I had not seen him arrive but his presence was announced by a general removal of headgear. 'I will inform the current minister. This is a grave situation,' he added. 'It's not impossible he may consider it necessary to bring one of these bodies to Berlin, to examine it in more detail.' Jakob, Altmayer and I exchanged glances, but it was Altmayer who was obliged to speak. 'We're not sure what to do with all these bodies. And there are more than a dozen soldiers from other, recognisable, forces, in the other pits, sir.' 'I have been informed. I don't know what you think, Mayor Altmayer, as the region's highest authority, but perhaps the decision rests with poor Redo, who owns the land.' 'With the decisive mediation of pastor Stein, who had to leave on ecclesiastical business a while ago.' 'Were the soldiers Christians?' A charged silence followed. 'What we have is a most thorny problem, jurisdictional, juridical, religious and even moral in nature,' Jakob said, brushing aside his thin hair. The dead bodies were gleaming; we living ones, in our dark clothes, resembled shadows. I took the liberty of intervening. *Sirs, with the greatest respect, I agree with Moltke and want to emphasise that I will not take any decisions without the complete agreement of the civil and ecclesiastical authorities. I want to be respectful towards my new fellow citizens, and likewise considerate towards these poor lads who, unfortunately for them and for me, met death or burial in this place.* 'An honourable resolution, Redo,' the Baron said on behalf of everyone. *Having said that, I'm sure you'll understand that my survival depends on starting to cultivate as soon as possible, and so I implore you all that we reach a joint decision without delay.* They nodded at each other. 'I will send a message by post to the Prefect this very night,' Altmayer said.[3] Geoffman nodded. 'The four of us will need to meet at some point over the following days, Baron: yourself, the Prefect, Stein and I, to formulate a joint, duly considered recommendation to Mr Hauptshammer. If the learned Mr Moltke wants to make a suggestion, it will be more than welcome.' I believe this was the first time anyone had referred to me as *Mister*. The truth is, no one in Prussia yet knew how to address the free peasants. Naturally, I did not object. The baron then gave me some more unexpected news, positive this time, shedding light upon so much darkness. 'Tomorrow I will bring you a cow on loan and two slaughtered lambs, Redo, so that you can sustain yourself during this period.' I thanked him enthusiastically for his generosity, because

---

3 Hauptshammer relates the facts for the second time, with light discrepancies. (Translator's note)

I was sincerely beginning to worry about my situation. The meeting was ended by Jakob, who looked at the exposed tombs and said: 'The land is a like a book: once open, it too can speak.'

Nobody had anything to add and we parted in silence.

The following days were turbulent; with Hans's help I covered the bodies back up, just enough so that they weren't exposed, and marked them with another cross; I had to extend the cabin on one side because the ox and the cow arrived almost at the same time, and Hans advised I keep them inside so they would not get cold and would warm the place up; I made a space for the hens, the cockerel and the tools, finding a space for Odra's coffin wherever I could; I oriented the wooden beams depending on whether they were from the base or close to the top on account of the dampness of the cabin wall, also according to Hans's instructions, since dampness in trunks rises but does not descend; I roasted one of the lambs and gutted and salted the other so that the meat would not spoil; I familiarised myself with the yoke and the plough; I reinforced the walls of the hut from the inside and outside, covering them with an insulating varnish Hans had given me; I milked the cow and began experimenting with cheesemaking – the initial results were either interrupted or disastrous – and as soon as I made a decent one I took half of it to my neighbour; I fed the animals and waited in vain for the hens to lay, since they still had not got used to their new, noisy home, and the cockerel wasn't in the mood yet; I passed the hours with such occupations, marked by sorrowful thoughts about Odra's absence, and many whinnies, moos and clucks. *At least I've got company,* I thought. I did occasionally have to open a window because between the smells of the animals' effluvia and their body odours the air within my home had become unbearably saturated. I also attended the tavern some evenings, to drink beer with Hans or Jakob or with gruff old Wreech if they weren't there. They all lamented my bad luck, although I kept trying to change the subject. On the holy day I went to the small church to hear the bells, so that no one could say I did not attend. I sat myself down, almost at the back, but in a visible spot so that I would be noticed by the pastor Stein and the authorities. Baron Geoffman and his angelic daughter Johanna entered the church through the back door, reserved exclusively for them, and sat in their own place, to one side of the central nave, next to the altar, separated with a gated wooden fence from the benches used by the other townspeople. Altmayer and Genoveva Ulmer sat on the first bench.

I have just remembered a conversation I had with the baron, months after all this, at the start of my second year in Szonden, and I'd like to note it down, for my memory sometimes offers me food that rots and disintegrates if I do not ingest it rapidly. I shall write it down here and find a more appropriate place for it later. The conversation takes place in the baron's study, beneath another portrait of his beloved spouse; we're finishing the contract for my services, agreeing on the annual sum. At that moment, an idea takes hold of me. I think about the remuneration we've discussed and double it in my head, confirming that the numbers add up and the total figure may well be enough for my new scheme. I take a gamble and propose it to Geoffman: *Baron, I agree with the amount in exchange for my work, under the terms agreed. But I want to vary the form of pay.* 'Do you want to be paid in advance, or for it to be underwritten by a bank?' *No, not at all, I'm not referring to that. I'm thinking about the annual sum. I believe I already know how much things cost in Oderbruch and have come up with an idea. My request is simple: I want you to pay me half of what we have agreed this coming year.* 'What's that? Half?' *Yes. And I want us to do the same the following year, you pay me 50% of that sum in talers.* 'I don't understand, Redo. If you hadn't had coffee I'd think you were drunk.' *In exchange for these two halves, which you will retain, at the end of next year I would like you to grant Hans a decree of free ownership for the land you own and on which he works as a tenant farmer.* The baron looks at me in shock. 'But, Redo... this proposal...' I can see that the numbers are already revolving in his head. I know when that happens because they are almost always moving around in mine too, and I tend to have that distant expression which is on the baron's face now; he tries to concentrate on his words, which express reticence and appeal to my proposal's lack of sense, but his mind is clearly thinking that it suits him; that, in reality, it's an advantageous move; over those two years he can get rent from the land and *at the same time*, get my services at no added cost; he calculates that Hans's land, a half horseshoe like mine, would imply no loss to him, given the extent of his land; he imagines that, even if he surrenders the land, he will be able to come to a concrete agreement with Hans in exchange for the handover, so that he will still come and work for him occasionally, since he places a high value on Hans's knowledge of agricultural chemistry gained from reading books in his spare time and successfully applying them to the soil; his mouth tries to dissuade me but his number-filled eyes say *yes*, and I know what always happens when two people both know that the numbers add up: the numbers speak through them and use their bodies like instruments; the eyes compel the mouth and eventually, despite opposition, the positive response spills out: 'Yes, Redo, I accept your offer. You are very magnanimous with Hans, he will be most grateful to you.' *It is I who am indebted to Hans and to yourself; all three of us know that without your generosity I would not have survived in Szonden.*

On one of those mornings in the early days, Jakob came to my land with a stranger. I was on the more elevated part of the plot from which you could make out the lower plain, with the cabin to the left of it and beyond it the river bank and then the Oder, the sun sparkling on its partially frozen surface. Once they were closer and I could see them better I deduced from the cut and quality of the clothes Jakob's companion was wearing that he must be powerful. And he was: the King's Justice Counsel, no less, visiting incognito to find out what was happening on my land. 'Counsel Franz Reitman is a friend of mine and when I mentioned this affair to him he didn't hesitate to come and see for himself, in a personal capacity.' I greeted him and we had a brief conversation; I uncovered a couple of frozen warriors for him, from different pits, and he was just as astonished by these lugubrious discoveries as the others had been. Jakob was filling him in on antecedents in the region's military history. 'If we could fly over these fields like birds, dear Franz, we would see that this region is full of craters created by artillery or the excavation of trenches and common graves for soldiers; these openings have been gradually disguised by vegetation and by erosion from the wind and rain, but if you were to remove all the plants and trees the area would be as pockmarked as the visible face of the moon.' The counsel nodded and expressed his wish that the wars against the Napoleonic empire were the last that would ever devastate Prussia.

As they talked, I saw that a white figure had stopped on one of the paths running along the boundary. I couldn't see who it was from that distance but the whiteness of her profile and her uncommon stillness, cut against the wood behind her, startled me. Then I remembered that unsettling white woman with red eyes whom I had crossed paths with one night while walking home from the inn. I glanced at Jakob, who looked towards the figure. 'That's Ilse, the strange woman who lives alone on the outskirts of Szonden. They call her Ilse the witch; some say she sees things.' 'Things?' Reitman inquired. 'Things,' Jakob replied mysteriously, returning his gaze to one of the frozen corpses. Reitman also turned and looked down into the open pit, his hands on his hips. 'The moon is the only place on the planet free of bloodshed,' the Counsel said suddenly. *How could it not be, if it is not part of the earth.* 'Exactly,' he responded and, as Jakob kept a pensive silence, I perceived that understanding the German mind would take longer than I had predicted. 'These fields are the fruit of the great king's colonisation, isn't that so, Jakob?' 'I don't know why you continue to hold that man in such high esteem, Franz. When we speak of the great king, Redo, we are referring to Frederick William II of Prussia,' Jakob commented as he turned towards me, and I was grateful for his explanation, without which I would have become even more lost. 'That man cut short more Prussian and foreign lives than cancer and heart attack combined in the entire 18th century. His lethal skills were only surpassed by that dangerous madman, Napoleon. A fine couple they cut, dancing their dance of death.' 'But Jakob...' 'My grandfather, who commanded a hussar regiment in those days, once saw that pig with his own eyes, sleeping like a log on the 12th August, 1759.' 'That was the day of the battle of Kunersdorf, wasn't it?' 'Indeed it was. It's not a date we can easily forget, for in the days following the battle the king took refuge nearby, in Reitwein. You can't imagine how terrible Kunersdorf was, Redo. By nightfall on that fateful day our army had lost 18,000 combatants on the battlefield. Eighteen thousand dead Prussians plus an equal number of Cossacks and two thousand Austrians, your countrymen. Between ten and fifteen thousand Prussian families lost one or more members because of the Enormous King's ineptitude. Do you think he lost any sleep over it? Do you think almost 40,000 corpses kept him awake at night, wracked with guilt and remorse over his clumsy strategic decisions? Absolutely not, that swine slept the sleep of the just; my grandfather saw him with his own eyes, snoring like a piglet on a heap of straw, his hat covering his face so that the light of history would not wake him. How can someone sleep so deeply after amassing a mountain of dead human beings and horses, which took days to remove from the fields? Do you remember how in Borodino the Russians and French sacrificed an entire company of soldiers each minute because Napoleon, who was suffering from high fevers, attacked the enemy head on? Did neither the Giant King nor the Excessive Emperor possess souls? Had they no wooden chessboards to play at hecatombs with? What are those wretches, the ones we allow to rule us, made of?' Counsel Reitman, who had become more and more nervous as Jakob's speech grew more indignant, gave the historian a severe look on his face and raised his index finger to reprimand him, looking around to make sure that no one else could hear, before saying in a low, hoarse voice: 'Causing a scandal is not the best way to change things, Jakob.' 'I'm sorry. Please, my friends, forgive me, I beg you. There is just so much insanity that I cannot understand...' 'Easy, my friend, one step at a time.' 'You're right, Franz, I'll be quiet. I will only say that the great king, as you call him, could be reproached with Arideo's words to Philotas in Lessing's play: "You will overwhelm your people with laurels and with misery. You will count more victories than happy subjects."' The counsel was still unsettled and clearly eager to change the subject. 'I do not understand what is happening on your land, Mr...' *Hauptshammer.* 'Hauptshammer, yes. But Jakob will keep me abreast of everything. If there's anything I can do for you from Berlin, let me know.' *I am most grateful, sir. My only wish is to work my land in peace.* 'That is what we want for all citizens, that each one may live their life in peace. We'll do everything possible.' Then he left. I looked towards the spot where white Ilse had been standing, but she had evaporated into thin air.

Sometimes I travel back in time, since I have many hours in which to do so. One of the moments I often return to is the first night. I barely noticed her when she arrived; she came in with two other young girls, all three of them thin, hungry, bedraggled. I gave them the relevant instructions, not entirely sure if they understood me or not, since two of them looked like foreigners; I showed them their bathroom, the same one for all three, then drew a bath and instructed the servant to bring them clean clothes and bring them there to wash. While they were washing, I prepared some food on the fourth floor and it was then, when Odra entered the kitchen after her bath, that I saw her properly for the first time. She was as thin as a rake, with big, hard eyes and dark brown skin and she moved like an undulating bow, in a way that marked out her foreign origins from a mile away. Austrians slide; she swayed. An implausible angel born in the contradiction between her thinness and the curvature of her movements. A nightgown that had been used by a hundred bodies before hers hung from her collarbone, leaving her squalid shoulders on display. She looked at me with curiosity from behind her sunken eyes as I handed her the hot goulash my mother had been taught how to cook by her bohemian relatives from Pardubice. After the second spoonful she looked at me again with gratitude and muttered the only Spanish word I knew, *gracias*. Though she did not speak our language, she knew the universal language of establishments such as ours. Her arms were two shoots sprouting from her white sleeves, moving nervously, at random. She seemed uncomfortable about her youth and beauty, unsure what to do with them, hiding

69

them as if wishing they would fade and she might become invisible. As she was too attractive to allow that,
she thought that by getting thinner she would be less
visible because she occupied less space in others' fields
of vision. But I could not get her out of mine. The other
two girls came in. They were blonde, a little more rotund and curvy; when I examined them I thought they
would bring us more money than the Spanish girl, but
I was wrong. She spied on me looking at the other two,
detecting that there was more mathematics than lasciv-
iousness in my eyes. I looked at her again and she must
have noticed the difference, although she arrogantly held
my gaze, lacking any hope or fear. I took the instruments
of inspection. It was not necessary to explain anything
to her. Without stopping eating, holding the bowl in one
hand and the spoon in the other, she turned on her seat
and opened her legs. When I knelt down in front of her
and took out the instruments, she gave me a devastating
look. Trusting, as if she knew she was in good hands, that
nothing bad could come from me. In that place, with that
look, at that moment, she bewitched me forever. We were
both as young as each other. I fell in love, knowing that
I shouldn't. Fully aware that she had come to our house,
to our place of business, to sleep with other people. The
other girls laughed when they saw my spellbound expression. She just smiled lightly, sweetly. The taller
blonde, who barely lasted a month, threw a piece of bread
at my head. I had to stand up and raise my voice to remind her who was in charge. I took away the plate of food
from the hussy who had thrown the bread and tipped its
contents into the bin. She started shouting. Without too

much force, since girls with bruised faces are no good to us, I slapped her to make her understand her place in the world: a florin-an-hour whore in a Vienna brothel in the early 19th century. A tense silence followed. Luckily, at that moment my mother arrived and the shrieking blonde sat down in a huff. My mother pointed at her and said 'Mimi'. She pointed to the other girl, after looking at her, and chose 'Elise'. And, finally, looking at my bony beloved, she said 'Odra'. And with no further words my mother marched off down the stairs, making her second-hand French boots resound against the wood.

Over the following days in Szonden, I was foaming at the mouth with rage; my impatience did not allow me to enjoy a situation which would perhaps have been enviable to many: living without working. Yes, I had food, fresh milk, salted meat and finally managed to curdle something resembling a decent cheese, but whenever I left the cabin to be confronted with the unhealthy sight of an uncultivated field, partially covered in snow and with several gloomy crosses placed haphazardly on its edges, I despaired. I pulled up weeds to do something productive. I was burning with desire to begin my new existence, to work in earnest, to bury Odra's coffin and distract myself with different occupations and not think or remember too much. But everything brought me back to her. Anything, any noise, any image, extracted her from my memory and deposited her in my eyes, in my skin, on my tongue, to a distressing degree. Those first nights, safe in the knowledge that no one could hear me, I cried years' worth of tears, almost shouting them out, because I knew that the mourning would have to pass far quicker than in other circumstances. I would have to overcome my grief like a sturdy Prussian peasant, which was just what I had become. Sometimes I laughed between the tears, thinking of the play I was staging against my will, at once dramaturg and tortured protagonist. If someone had described it for me just four years earlier I wouldn't have believed it, since I never imagined myself outside of Vienna, continuing in my mother's unpredictable line of work. But now I had a dignified life ahead of me, or, rather, I would soon: it was there, before my eyes, but the cursed corpses had delayed everything by erecting a fence between expectation and reality. And that was devouring me.

So one of those mornings I went out for a walk, as if I were a rich man with no occupation who could permit himself to wander while others toil. I took a large stroll around the outskirts of the town, since I did not feel like greeting anyone or talking about the news or the sad affair of my farm, to the other edge of Szonden, which I hadn't visited yet. It's an area marked out by the first signs of the nearby Schmargendorf forest, which thickens after a few hundred metres. The vegetation surrounding me was portentous and the day, though cold, was clear, which meant that the sun lit up the treetops in explosions of green. The walk, which regulates the organs and glands and soothes inner demons, lifted my spirits and without feeling at all fatigued, I reached an imposing mill which some townspeople had mentioned to me. The building was next to a small stream flowing into the Oder, from whose force the enormous red wood blades extracted their gyratory force. The mill tower was also a vivid red, so much crimson colliding with the surrounding green, like a bloody wound on a frog's skin. I approached it, thinking I could buy a sack of flour, or a cheese superior to my homemade efforts, when I came across the miller, whose hips swayed hypnotisingly as she approached me. Jakob, I then remembered, had spoken about her. 'Hello, you must be Redo, the newcomer. I'm Ingeborg.' Until that moment I would have sworn that my body was dead and no sensation could stir it after Odra's death; if only an hour or a day earlier you had told me that I would be capable of feeling any kind of arousal I would have laughed bitterly, thinking that nothing in the world could make me feel alive. But the shapely forms which Ingeborg's clothing struggled to contain as she carried a sack of hay over her left shoulder and held out her right hand to me generated a strange electric shock which did not rise above my belly button but made my nether regions almost tremble, devastated by the firm curves before me. My conscious part felt a kind of block, half surprised and half terrified by the earthquake my subconscious was enduring. Young Ingeborg's blue eyes, outlined by some unruly curls escaping from her tied-up red hair, and above all, her bright red lips, which possessed a plumpness and thickness I had never before known and which curved into a half-open smile, created telluric heat waves that spread downwards while my frozen mind and my dead heart could not understand one jot of what was happening to their southern part, from my stomach to the soles of my feet. Bodies possess no memory or feelings of guilt, they neither recount life's wounds nor suffer its low points. I don't know if I said anything; I may have stammered out a few words. I felt a deep anger towards that part of me which could neither contain itself nor respect my mourning, however beautiful and seductive the figure I had before me was, blessed with a bulging bust which could be partly made out through the upper part of the blouse, whose tulle borders allowed a glimpse of a curved watercourse of beauty with a few beads of sweat tumbling down it, resisting the cold due to their owner's physical labour; I made an effort not to look but to speak. The situation could not have been more frustrating, because I hadn't the slightest idea of what I was saying and my inner Helmut and Peter were howling and grunting, demanding nature follow its course. Thankfully tiny Regina, wisely silencing the other molecular voices and reminding my other parts, selves and excited glands and organs that I could not, *in any way*, talk or act in an uncontrolled manner and risk revealing myself and losing everything I'd achieved so far, and once more I blessed that tiny portion of my psyche which managed to impose sense in the midst of that chaotic whirlwind of heat and desire that were already ravaging the lower two thirds of my body, allowing an excuse to escape from my mouth: *What an idiot! I came to buy something but I've forgotten my money.* I put kilometres of distance, deserts of time and oceans of space between myself and that sinuous portent of nature. Despite Ingeborg's friendly shouts, rapidly fading in volume due to the speed of my flight, assuring me that money wasn't necessary, that she could trust me, asking why was I leaving so quickly, had she said or done something which might have annoyed me, the poor thing, what an enchanting woman, what a nightmare of

74

a woman, I fled her dominions like a soul being taken by the devil – something I was all too familiar with – promising to never again set foot in this part of Szonden. At least not until a few years had passed. Or a year, I was unfamiliar with local mourning customs. Or six months, if it was in secret, nothing less. I was so nervous when I got back to the farm that I ran in, literally, as fast as my legs would carry me and, sweating and not sure what to do with my body, I closed the door and embraced Odra's coffin, begging her for forgiveness, though I had not actually done anything.

Then, while the upper part of my body wept and the lower part struggled to control itself, I realised I had to bury Odra immediately. It was impossible to live like that.

The following day, I headed to Altmayer's house on 14 Oderstrasse, intending to ask him if the meeting of the various authorities agreed upon a few days ago had taken place. His door was opened by Utta, who told me that the mayor had gone out on business in Kunowice and would return in the evening. In the back, Mrs Ulmer was sitting by the chimney, completely absorbed in shining some leather boots with a worn-out cloth. After brushing her hair from her face, lowering her voice and suddenly abandoning the discretion and timidity she had deployed in Altmayer's presence, she expressed her condolences for my wife's death, told me not to worry, that I had a sweet face and a very interesting beard – those were her exact words – and that before long there would be no shortage of women in Oderbruch with whom I could recover my future – those were her words – and once more I had the urge to flee, though not as much as I had before the toned flesh of Ingeborg the miller, whose memory I had tried to shoo from my dreams during the previous night, without too much success. As I turned, Utta recommended I visit Mr Jakob, because the historian had been at the meeting of notables – that's what she called it – and told me that his house was the last one on the adjoining street and that he left that house every day to take a break from working and buy some pastries, at this exact hour. I turned towards her with my most grateful expression, looked down and removed my woollen cap. When I looked up again she had already closed the door.

Would I ever understand Germans?

But on the other hand, isn't it just as inexplicable that I should be writing this story now, so many years later, the way I am writing it? Is my contradiction any easier to understand than the German soul, at once metaphysical and earthly?

I took the adjoining street, following the directions of unfathomable Utta, whose sinewy slenderness vaguely reminded me of Odra's svelte form, and, once again, I was blinded by the sunlight that reflected from the white walls and the windows of the houses, which encouraged me to keep going, to refuse to be defeated by sadness, to keep fighting, to strive to live. The cobblestones were partially covered in snow, the street was as white as the flour in the bakery which Jakob was leaving exactly then, holding a small package of pastries, just as Utta had predicted. He was pleased to see me and did not need to be cajoled; after he had sincerely reached out his hand for me to shake he offered to take me on a walk so that we could discuss the previous day's meeting.

'Redo, I won't try to deceive you, the issue we're facing is most thorny,' he said. As the package was visibly hindering his walking, he opened it and we ate the pastries between the two of us, so that at the beginning of the conversation our tongues were gummy with sugar and milled almonds. We walked down several streets at ease, Jakob talking quietly and calmly, greeting men he knew with a hand gesture, women with a nod, his body swaying a little towards both sides as he went forward, unable to balance it because his hands were placed reflectively behind his back. From time to time, at more serious moments, he would place his hand on my shoulder for a few instants to express proximity and support. I would certainly be lucky if that man became my friend, I thought. 'That's not the only thing,' he continued after the preliminaries, as we circled the ancient military fort, vanquished by ivy, snow and shrubs. 'We are concerned about potential interference from Berlin, although my friend Franz, to whom I introduced you on your land...' – *Yes, I remember* – 'is doing everything possible to maintain impartiality over there. Ah look, what a coincidence, here comes Stein.' 'Gentlemen.' *Vice-rector, good day.* 'Good day. I'm sorry I can't join you on your walk, I'm expected within the hour at Frankfurt von Oder and still must carry out two confessions...' 'We have it under control, my friend.' 'Are you informing Redo about the...' 'Yes.' 'You should know, my new and esteemed neighbour, that we wish to resolve this issue as soon as possible.' *I'm truly grateful.* 'And as soon as I am able I will come and visit you, to

77

speak at more leisure. Good day.' 'Goodbye, Stein.' The vice-rector left at full speed, his cape unleashing from the ground a storm of leaves and snowflakes. *You were saying; everyone has the best intentions, but...* 'Yes, but we will have to wait for the Prefect to inform Berlin and then return. There are always objections whenever two administrations join. And, in this case, two eras: the past one, represented by Geoffman and the new one, symbolised by you, Szonden's first free farmer. Two regimes, two ways of seeing the state and the world. This complicates everything more than the bureaucratic processes in themselves. The problem is how to form a *vision* concerning things. Before, that vision came directly from above: if the king did not formulate it, the prince electors would; if not them, the ministers, archbishops and nobles; in their absence, bishops or prefects or counsels, and so on and so on in a way that was tiered, hierarchical and indisputable. Now no one is sure where to start with minor, local matters. I understand that it should be horizontal, but those who cling onto the old structures, like the Baron or Mayor Altmayer, think that the old regime must and can persist, in diluted form, into the new one, adapted to the new state of things. Both I and, strangely, Stein have a different belief.' I noticed that Jakob wanted to elaborate but, unsure if I could express my suspicions aloud and encourage him to keep talking, I opted for something in between, with the aim of continuing to talk about the same subject. *For some time now, there have been tensions in France similar to those you describe, and they were solved by greater control from above and less control from below. The Emperor could be as absolute as the Sun King regarding questions of State, yes,*

*but in my time there I noticed that Napoleon showed genuine
liberality towards the lower classes, if only because they didn't
concern him much.* 'That's what I mean, Redo,' said Jakob,
pointedly lowering his voice and looking around him. 'It's
about deciding if the state is there to order or to impose
order. The two terms seem almost equal, but they're not
the same thing. We,' he said, without clarifying who was
included in that *we*, 'think that there is no problem there
being a king if there is also a legislative assembly, demo-
cratically elected, to relieve his majesty of the heavy, both-
ersome load of governing the kingdom and allow him to
dedicate himself to court celebrations, military parades
and Italian operas.' He stopped abruptly and looked at me
to observe my reaction. To know who he was standing
in front of. *The other day I told one of Geoffmann's lackeys
that on my field I have neither master nor lord.* Jakob smiled,
came closer and gave me an embrace which I returned
the way I always do to avoid close contact: pushing my
elbow against the other person's torso, and enthusiastically thumping their back so that the other person does
not doubt my affection. To put it simply, I could not hug
like them. I had to keep control over my mind, voice and
body at all times. With that embrace, the beginning of our
friendship was sealed, I can see that clearly now. *However,
Jakob, something tells me that I must be cautious, that I must
not take the decision alone, so I am inclined towards whatever decision you reach... so long as it coincides with my own
wishes.* We both laughed freely; Jakob had a deep, boom-
ing chuckle, which rebounded off the trees of the nearby
Schmargendorf forest. This suddenly reminded me of the
miller Ingeborg, her mill and her fleshy lips weren't far

79

from there and I felt terror. *I'd like to go back to where we came from, I have some chores to do in town.* 'Of course.'

On the way back, Jakob told me some stories from his youth and seemed content. I let him talk so as not to interrupt him since, unfortunately, I could not do the same. I became aware of something: if I was going to have friends in Szonden I had to invent for myself a past full of coherent details. To that end, Odra and I were always clear that it would be necessary to write. Big, complex lies can only sustain themselves if they are backed up by an immutable text to return to from time to time, to remember the finer details. If memory is unreliable, invention is even more ductile and treacherous. That gave me an idea, which took shape as Jakob was speaking. 'In those times I was more fun. I had a gift for science and I was a Liebniz fanatic. I even began a new religion with some fellow students, in which God was mathematical exactitude and the saints were prime numbers. We were almost put to death for it, but we enjoyed ourselves a great deal.' Jakob smiled and raised his hat to scratch his head. I noted how his flesh vibrated from his waist to his arm, quivering with age and fat, proving to me that age operates on beings the way time works on nature, that adiposities are to people what humus is to the earth, covering once-firm skins and rocks, and that both are signals of long, fruitful lives rather than signs of decay; earlobes and nails that grow and drop and drooping breasts are like the branches of old trees, gradually worn down by weight and the passing seasons. Old people are thin and small because they've given all of themselves, like fruit falling to the earth and fertilising it with its substrate.

At that moment I saw an extremely tall, almost inhuman figure, on the edge of a cultivated field. I couldn't quite see but imagined it was the giant, Udo. I mentioned it to Jakob, who asked if I knew him, to which I replied, *more or less*. 'Udo is a local phenomenon, every now and then he is visited by doctors from nearby regions, and once a year a carriage from the Berlin Faculty of Medicine comes to collect him so that its students can examine him.' *How tall is he?* 'No one knows exactly. Every year it's different. Some years he's shorter, others a foot taller...' *How is that possible.* 'That's why they take him to Berlin, to try and solve the mystery. I tell you, he's a phenomenon. And that's not the only strange thing.' *What do you mean?* 'Right now, as you will see, he is gathering the honey from that comb...' *I can't see in detail from here; I guessed it was Udo but I can't make out what he's doing.* 'He removes the combs from the hive and extracts the honey. The strange thing is he needs neither bee suit nor gloves. The bees don't bite him.' *And that's strange?* He looked intently at me. 'But, Redo... I suggest you go with him and see for yourself. Once you get within three metres of it you will get stung hundreds of times. Usually beekeepers approach the hive with burning grass in their hands, the greener the better, so that the smoke disperses the insects and keeps them away long enough to extract the honey. No one in their right mind would approach a beehive without some such tactic. It's clear you haven't been a country person for long.' *I had no idea.* 'Szonden beekeepers feed Udo in exchange for his work, every day he eats in a different house and lives off a small income which his mother left to Wreech so that he would feed him whenever he visits the tavern. Udo is the last remaining man with no knowledge of money. He has never used it and does not understand the concept, more from unwillingness than anything else. The poor thing may lack intelligence but he's no idiot.' I remembered the first time I saw him, the day of my arrival in the town, telling me I was *strange*. At that precise moment the giant turned to look at us and I felt something resembling an icy finger on my spine. We kept walking, leaving him to his work.

'Prussia is a difficult place and for a while it was grey and cruel, but there is space in it for imagination and beauty,' Jakob said, looking melancholically at the green forest surrounding us, next to the milestone just before the first houses in Szonden. 'Although the supposedly *new* ideas espoused by those young romantics merely conceal greater political and religious reactionism than that which already exists, it cannot be denied that they have understood the artistic possibilities of these valleys, their mystery, their uncommon beauty, the layers of legend which form them like the strata of humus does the soil. I don't like their ideas but I do like their poems.' *I haven't read them, Jakob. Which spurs me to ask you a favour.* 'Granted.' *I'd like you to polish my writing; I can write, but poorly; I'd like to have more notions of grammar, syntax, style...* Jakob thought quickly. 'That can be done. It will be simple because you have a good grasp of the structures in your head, you speak clearly and with surprising detail. One thing... I'll have to consult with Stein.' *Stein.* 'Yes, I know, it's irritating but anything to do with education goes through him.' I was annoyed by that filter. I rolled my mental dice. *What if we met two or three times a week at Wreech's tavern and you bring some books and tell everyone that you've had problems with cramps in your hands and you've taken me on as a temporary amanuensis to put your work to paper.* Jakob looked at me in surprise. 'That's Machiavellian, sardonic, perfect.' *I only understood the last word, and that's precisely what we must correct.* Jakob let out another raucous laugh, the piercing tones of which could be heard at once by Hans and the miller Ingeborg, a league apart. 'It's a deal, what a magnificent solution. So, if all goes well, you will be your own hired labourer, the baron's accountant and my private secretary.' *Yes, unfortunately. I need to do many things to avoid thinking about my own affairs.* Jakob understood, took my shoulder and guided me towards the centre of town, explaining how we would organise the lessons masquerading as dictation sessions. At some point we walked past Johanna, Baron Geoffman's daughter, previously glimpsed fleetingly in her mansion, ascending the same hill we were descending, accompanied by her housekeeper, Mrs Wolff. Johanna greeted Jakob with a nod, which he returned, and to everyone's surprise, when we were almost level with one another she said 'Good morning, Mr Hauptshammer,' piercing me with her green eyes in a way that would have finished off any living being, animal or vegetable, male or female, except, luckily, myself, as her gaze was directed at my head and my heart, both of which were blinded at that moment by the abiding memory of Odra. Any dart not aimed at regions below the belly button was harmless because my soul was elsewhere, like Saint Sebastian's as the arrows pierced him. Once he was a few paces away from the lady and her housekeeper, he commented slyly: 'But Redo, that beard of yours and your thin figure are wreaking more havoc than all the muscles and shaved faces of the lads in the Old March.' *It's just because I'm new and different.* 'Well, I fear that now every man in Szonden is going to want to change their skin and arrive from afar.' We laughed. We talked and laughed. We conversed and laughed. Thus it continued, for almost three decades.

And it's not only friendship I owe him. Some years after the facts I related, I can't remember how many exactly, Jakob sent a girl to my house with a message that I was to come urgently. I ran to his house, thinking he might have a serious health problem, but his excited state was in response to something else: he had a guest. 'Actually, there are two of them, but her husband doesn't count,' he whispered as I approached the living room, where there were two people who, by their clothes and bearing, had to be important. And they were. He was a diplomat, Karl August Varnhagen von Ense, whom Jakob introduced to me as a fundamental part of the team that had accompanied Hardenberg to the Vienna Congress. The woman, who had fascinating black eyes, a sharp nose and hair graciously gathered into three ponytails, began to speak without waiting to be introduced by Jakob: 'Don't believe a word of what that bookworm says about us; he'll bore you about how we've been friends with Goethe and Grillparzer and say we're some snooty Gallicised Berliners, but none of that is true. In fact, Börne, Heine and Grillparzer, among others, are our amanuenses, and we dictate our books to them because our modesty impedes us from seeking renown.' I kissed her hand, not knowing what to say. Her husband had a smile I would later interpret as his main diplomatic tool, and Jakob laughed one of his characteristic guffaws, in C major, the acoustic power of which must have filled the entire Oderbruch with waves of interlinked Hs and Os. The woman was Rahel Varnhagen, one of the fastest and most exceptional minds of her time. 'You're surprisingly good looking for a Wiener, Redo,' she added. 'Are you sure you're Austrian? Say something in your language.' This time even her husband, used to her witticisms, had to laugh. 'In 1815 we spent a season in Vienna, and we felt so decadent we decided to read Chateaubriand's *Atala*, imagine our embarrassment recalling it now. We have not set foot in your country since, lest cheap exoticism assault us. How did you get that beard? Dear Karl, if you had a beard like that we wouldn't socialise so often.' The whole evening was more or less like that; Rahel worked her magic and we watched the spectacle of her uninterrupted speech, unfurled towards us like a magic lantern of intelligence. When I had a firm grip on writing and was having genuinely intelligent thoughts I asked Jakob for her address, and until Rahel's death I kept up a correspondence with her. What an extraordinary woman, enviable in so many ways. The days when her incisive manuscripts arrived were the highlights of every month. That epistolary friendship, precious since it gained me a tiny place in the world of ideas, I also owe to Jakob.

The morning after the walk with Jakob, during which he informed me that I would have to continue to wait for the solution to my problem, I woke up with a tremendous headache. I had made two mistakes the night before: spending too much time at the tavern with Hans, drinking one wine after another, and then continuing to drink when I got back to my cabin, saddened by the company of Odra's coffin. I needed to decide, but instead of that I decanted two skeins of wine and let myself go. I failed at forgetting, instead remembering with great intensity, the images lacking precision and yet beating me as if with a club. I even suffered a momentary bout of madness in which I thought about removing the lid to embrace Odra and make love to her remains. Fortunately, that atrocious thought did not outlast the moment.

At dawn I felt enormous confusion, both physical and spiritual, through which only one idea shone bright: bury the casket and start a new life. I fed the beasts, cleaned the cabin, collected the eggs the hens were finally laying and, after a meagre snack, went out into the cold to clear my head. It had snowed. My land was completely white again, the dawn light interrupted only by the sinister crosses. In the distance, there seemed to be a vague, grey dot on one of the paths. As I approached, it turned out to be two dots, one white and one shorter and darker. Getting closer, I saw that the light blur was the witch Ilse, an albino dressed in a white coat, next to an enormous dog, although I couldn't make out the breed from that distance. Ilse left him on the path and walked towards me, treading through the snow. 'Stay there, Delto,' she ordered the dog. *He's enormous*, I said, to open the conversation. But Ilse did not wish to chat about the animal; pointing at the wooden crosses in order, she said: 'I knew that one's daughter. Those ones are French. Those four are from the New March, when it was still Polish. Those ones aren't from here, they're from the past. And those sixteen aren't from here nor the past.' *Where are they from, then?* 'The question is not where, but when.' *So... when are they from?* The witch stopped, fire glowing in her red eyes. The enormous dog made a guttural, cavernous, ancient noise. I shivered. 'There are more,' Ilse said, pointing to the central part of the plot. *Of course. There will be 32.* She turned to face me in shock. 'How can you know that? Are you also...' *No, my gift is with numbers. After the fourth coincidence it is not magic but rather a system.* I did not try to evade the fire in her red orbits. One might say that, just as moles can see in the darkness of the soil, Ilse could see through the darkness of time. *When are the other warriors from?* 'From all times, from diverse origins. They are all soldiers, save one from the future: a civilian, who will be a writer. Are you going to remove them?' *I don't know. I don't know what I'm going to do.* 'Delto and I know who you are. But don't worry, you're safe with us. Singular people need to look after each other.' I smiled. I felt a certain humanity in the embers of her eyes. I approached Delto to pet it, for I have always got on with dogs. The animal took to me, it could sense that I was no danger. But despite its favourable disposition, once I had reached its side I did not stroke it.

It was a wolf.

6

A. The completely white variety called Silesian gives great yields and is high in sugar. It's highly suited to these climes because its root sinks deep into the earth and it is resistant to both drought and frost. The day I decided to plant it, Hans told me that 'beet benefits from a fertiliser rich in calcium, phosphoric acid and potassium.' *Perfect, but where do I get them from? Lebus market?* Hans laughed. 'You get it from bone char, by burning animal bones and mixing them with the remains of dead animals like chickens, rats and cockerels, ground to a pulp. To this mixture you add dung from your ox and cow, which you must collect as if it was treasure – I strongly recommend doing it outside, if it's rotten then all the better. Any defecation from any animal, including your horse and yourself, should be kept, because they're worth their weight in gold. Chimney ash is also ideal for mixing with the other stuff. You must start gathering all these things soon because you have quite a lot of land and the fertiliser won't go as far as you think.' Shit as treasure, what an idea.

B. 'I see you haven't dug up the remaining bodies.' *No.* 'But they're there.' *I know.* 'Delto can smell them from the house, and he howls.' *What's the point in taking them out? I still haven't reached an agreement with the authorities regarding the others. Imagine I decide to bury them again – what's the use in unearthing them now?* 'They want to see the light.' *It's the same light as when they were alive. They won't enjoy it more now.* 'You're wise, that's rare these days.' *I'm just trying to survive.* 'I can see the future. Do you want to know your role in it?' *My future is like your past, Ilse, I can read both: in the best possible case it still consists of suffering. But we've got used to it, we're in our element now, aren't we? Some ray of light amid the slumber, that's enough to keep going. Yes, old woman, you see more than me, but you can't feel more than me. I know pain in the same intimate way the mother eagle knows her chicks, one by one, feather by feather. I can detect a resigned commitment to survival from afar, just as your wolf can smell the dead.*

C. 'Now, copy what I dictate, from Carl Gottlieb Svarez: "Forming a correct and perennially updated concept of the State's goals is a matter of the utmost importance, as much for the government as for its subjects. For the subjects, because by doing so they will slowly develop a voluntary and rational obedience towards their supreme leader and, by considering the advantages the state guarantees them and their fellow citizens, they can accept the various restrictions to which they submit, just as they do with the multiple daily sacrifices they must make for the benefit of that union."' *For the subjects, because... The things you make me copy.* 'You need to understand your new country. This is how it's worked for years. In any case, Austria isn't much better.' *You're right... Considering the advantages... isn't this sentence too long?* 'Yes, the parataxis is a little forced. The clumsy style lacks elegance. I'm pleased you noticed.' *What's the purpose in copying it?* 'Firstly, so you understand Prussia. Secondly, and more importantly, so you realise what hard work it is to write badly and how easy it is to write well. Wreech, two white beers, *s'il vous plaît.*'

D. *Johanna, you must leave the bedroom. Your father might come back at any moment.* 'This is my house, I'm allowed to be here.' *Not wearing those clothes, or rather, wearing so little; please, cover yourself.* 'There are eleven million people in Prussia and you're the only human being who doesn't devour me with your eyes.' *I'm not Prussian yet.* 'Does that mean I have some hope for the future?' *I need to get on with these accounts, Johanna, and your father will be back within minutes. Right now, the only future I'm contemplating is the three hours I still need to make these talers square. For the sake of your future dowry, that is in your interests.* 'I hope the dowry is for you. I want it all to be for you.' *Please, girl, do up that bodice, I want to go home and sleep without having to think about fighting a dawn duel with your father.*

These past conversations come back to me all mixed up, like birdsong in a forest.

Now, so many years later, different storylines fit into others, like shards of the same broken mirror. Back then, however, each thread was separating into a chaotic tangle, the multitude of frayed ends asphyxiating me.

I must continue to record those first weeks in Szonden, because it was then that the first part of my life ended and the current one began, and I need to put those days in writing so that I am able to retain the details without memory interfering. First, though, I'll skip forward a little.

That beet I planted some pages back will grow with gusto, demonstrating its superior quality compared with that cultivated in the Magdeburg Börde, thanks to the rich soil. This will bring me plentiful profits, allowing me to purchase a second ox and cow, and gradually, harvest by harvest, I will extract more and more profit, coming to agreements first with other producers in Szonden and then with a sizeable part of the Oderbruch, planting seeds from my beets and teaching others how to cultivate the crop in exchange for a percentage. Those percentages will allow me, over the years, to buy land while Johanna's husband, a pretentious Junker or landowner, as presumptuous as he is inept in business matters, whittles away the inheritance of the late Baron Geoffman, who will die four years after I arrive in Szonden. I will end up having a good relationship with the former lord, both professional and personal. Before dying, he will ask me if I desire any of his small possessions: his Triberg cuckoo clock, his gold Swiss quill, things like that.

I will ask for his glasses.

One night, during a village dance, twelve years after the baron's funeral, I will chance upon his son-in-law in a small wood, blind drunk, hitting a young girl who has resisted his advances. I won't do anything immediately, until I see that the girl has escaped. When he's alone, trying to crawl back onto the path, I'll cover my face and give him a good kicking, breaking three of his bones. I'll leave the bastard gasping and then I too will flee along the path. No one will discover anything and the authorities will determine that the assailant must have been from a nearby village, taking advantage of the commotion of the festival to rob the baroness's husband. Months later I will confess to Johanna. Far from being angry, she will hug and thank me.

Because, for understandable reasons, I have not been able to let myself have intimate relations with anyone in Szonden, I will use trips to Magdeburg, sometimes necessary for selling the fruits of my harvest or buying seeds, other times invented, to find a suitable brothel. Very few German brothels offer the services I require, and throughout all these years I have had to show extreme caution and discretion. Before arriving in Magdeburg, I always stop at a leafy crook by the Elba, where I change my clothes and disguise myself so that I am not recognised there. My unremarkable horse and carriage go completely unnoticed, as do I. I do my business, unburden myself and return to the same crook on the riverbank, where I resume my former appearance. Then I head home, armed with physical and mental calm for several months and a shipment of fresh images to recall at my convenience during the long, lonely nights.

Acclimatising to the town will take several years. My circumstances will make everything especially complicated. I will have to socialise without getting close to anyone. There are countless things that others do which I never can. I will never be able to bathe in the Oder by day, for example. I will always do it by night, alone, in silence, within my depth, with a pleasant mixture of fear and excitement when some fish or amphibian brushes past my thighs. I will never participate in the shooting competitions usually held around the harvest festival, blaming my poor sight. I will not be able to get drunk, instead drinking moderately and safely at home. Maintaining this isolation without seeming like a misanthrope or a madman will be complicated but I will achieve it using a thousand excuses, all work-related. Unfortunately, they will almost always be genuine, because I will work three thousand hours a year every year after I arrive in Szonden, divided between farming, accounting and organisation.

In thirty years, to this day, I will not kiss anyone in Szonden. There will be no kisses or embraces outside Magdeburg.

I will always have to control my behaviour, voice and language. I will never be able to be who I really am.

There will be a critical moment, involving Udo, when everything almost unravels because of one blasted coincidence. Perhaps I shall recall this episode further on. Luckily, the giant will see fit not to mention the incident, or if he does tell anyone then they will pay him no mind. Now, let us return to those early days.

I realise that at no point have I described the town of Szonden, another defect of the unexperienced narrator, I suppose. After Jakob's death I believed there was no point in writing anything, since he was the only reader in the town – the baron, a great lover of the Latin classics, had died long before. But over recent months I have come to realise this statement is untrue: I am the only reader in Szonden. So here is the description. It's simple: draw a small pentagon-shaped town square on a map; put a church to the far east and the council building opposite, to the west, on the other side of the shape. Six streets come off that square in every direction and then other circular streets unite the vertical ones in a radial shape, relative to the central square. Then, further away, sketch some allotments, small plantations, a couple of warehouses; to the west, the beginning of the Schmargendorf forest and Ingeborg's mill; to the north, the remains of the fortress; to the south, the road to Frankfurt von Oder and finally, to the east, the Oder itself, with most of the farms, among them Hans's and mine. In this little tangle of streets there are workshops, small businesses, glove shops, a seed shop, the tiny local chamber of commerce – which I will preside over for a few years – a bookshop that survived thanks to Jakob, the baron and Hans, then thanks to me, several grain warehouses, two dressmakers, a place to buy meat and cold cuts, two cheesemongers, an iron forge, an army office, a veterinary blacksmith, Stein's vice-rectory. The rest are typical *Giebelhaus* where the never numerous inhabitants of Szonden live.

That's it. The best place in the world.

Back then, however, I did not think of it like that, because the hell continued. I had begun ploughing the areas with no corpses. To begin with, I respected the zone where the thirty-two remaining bodies were buried, but later suspected they didn't care what happened above them; at the end of the day, they rested six feet beneath the crops.

I stopped looking for a definitive resting place for Odra in the exposed earth. One night I understood: to excavate was to attract more frozen soldiers, more horror. I knew that I would never free myself from my beloved, among other reasons because I did not wish to do so, it was obvious that she was the first and only woman in my life. There could never be another. Prostitutes had only ever moved my body. So I decided to bury her inside the house. I put a gravestone at the edge of the field, with her name engraved on it, to make my neighbours think she was buried there. In fact, Odra is beneath this very room, ten feet underground, not far from the chimney and a long way from the ice, so that she never suffers cold or freezes like the soldiers. By now she must be earth, like all that surrounds her. On that distant night, I did not think I could allow her body to become one more corpse, tossed into the cold night. She would always be inside the house, with me, as we had dreamt from the beginning.

Sometimes, tragically, we write the future ignorant of the consequences of not emphasising certain details. Inhabiting a space with another person can inevitably end with one or both being dead. As lovers, our imagination had never considered this macabre possibility. It imagined the story for us.

I couldn't stop looking at her during her first days in our brothel. Her movements were a slow spectacle, an opera interpreted by a single actress in which all the movements were carried out hesitantly and the protagonist, instead of singing, whispered inextricable Spanish words. She gathered her hair and hid it inside baggy clothes so as not to appear beautiful. My mother had to pursue her, to let her hair out and comb it for her. She forced me to dress her differently, and it was an incomparable delight for me to take her to the dressing room and choose her outfit, to remove her loose-fitting nightgown and slip her slim, brown limbs into tighter clothes. Her skin was soft and firm, and despite her thinness, her curves, especially her legs, stuck out sensually, inviting touch. I took advantage of the opportunity to touch her, my hands nervous and insecure, and she smiled, conscious of my embarrassment and desire. Male and female clients were wild about her. Everyone wanted a second go; once they'd spent time with Odra, as my mother baptised her, they no longer needed anyone else. Odra confessed to me that she preferred her female clients because they sought not to possess but rather enjoy her. When she told me what they did to her I was filled with rage and jealousy. It took time for me to reveal my feelings which, of course, went far beyond desire.

The first time I held her in my arms, kissing her, was identical to the last. A mirror image. One day she felt sick, and we feared she might have fallen pregnant. She hadn't, luckily, but still I took her to her room to rest. I closed the door and began undressing her. When her dress was down to her waist I noticed her looking at me in a different way. I put one knee on the ground, lowered her towards me, rested her back on my bent leg and kissed her slowly, first with my eyes closed, then open. Five years later, in Mainz, I gathered her up from the ground after the bullet which had entered through her back had exited through her chest; by the strange way she looked at me, I knew she couldn't even speak. I rested her on one leg, my other one resting on the ground, to kiss her for the last time. Our tears blending with our tongues.

I need a moment.

All right. I will erase these lines later, but I couldn't have just gone on writing.

A French soldier who had been incarcerated in a Mainz prison since returning from the Battle of Leipzig in 1813, a survivor, unfortunately, of the typhus epidemic of 1814, managed to escape, disarming a Prussian soldier. Rifle in hand, he reached the market where Odra and I were procuring provisions before continuing to Szonden. Two grenadiers spotted him and began shooting. In the crossfire, the crowd lost its mind and we began running without knowing if we were getting closer to or further away from the danger. A stray shot from the Frenchman hit Odra and ended our lives. I don't know what our last words to each other were. In the few seconds that remained between being hit and dying we could only kiss and cry.

Odra was the last victim of the war between France and the Sixth Coalition, years after the armistice had been signed.

As unnecessary and absurd a victim as all the others.

Jakob used to tell me about battles. He said that while human beings were given to occasional violence, almost always for geographical or economic reasons, societies were structurally peaceful. There was violence from above (disputes between countries over borders) and violence from below (disputes between neighbours over field boundaries), but the norm across the immense intermediary social sector is peaceful cohabitation. 'However,' he would add, 'over the last few decades we have witnessed a multiplication of violent conflicts that are difficult to comprehend, and bloodier and bloodier each time. If it continues like this,' he finished sarcastically, 'your field will end up seeming like a very small taster of the total war dead.' I didn't know whether to laugh or cry.

Jakob taught me history, stressing that it was a transcendental subject. 'Remember,' he commented one evening in Wreech's tavern, a few weeks after I arrived in Szonden, 'the importance of historiography in our trajectory as a culture. Men of state want to appear in those books, they think history manuals are the novels the gods read. Our dear Fritz, which is what they call the foolish Frederick II here, carried a volume of Plutarch during battles; uncouth Napoleon made notes in his edition of Machiavelli between battles, and emperor Marcus Aurelius consulted Greek manuscripts while keeping the Parthians and Sarmatians at bay. Alexander the Great received history classes throughout his long campaigns, doubtless to understand how he would come to take up his place in it. Kings and emperors take notes from their predecessors, seeing themselves as a senseless Council of the Elect which makes and transforms men's lives.' *Change is right. They destroyed mine.* 'They destroyed everyone's lives, Redo. Not all the victims are buried; war silently takes root in the lives of the survivors, castrating it, filling it with fear or poverty, limiting the common future.' *Do you think the wars in Europe are over?* 'I doubt it. There are too many small nations and earldoms, as well as three powers with aspirations of totality: Prussia, Austria and France. In Spain there's tension between liberals and absolutists (here too, though the latter are the overwhelming majority) and Italy is a mosaic of tiles which at some point someone will have to put together, we hope without resorting to fire and blood, but... And then there's the problem of the Balkans, which I fear will never be fixed. There comes a moment, Redo, when the excess of past is as harmful as the lack of it. There's too much history in the Balkans. It's impossible to move with that burden on your shoulders.' *What might happen here, then?* 'In theory, and despite the efforts some of us are making, I fear things won't change much. The university is not as well regarded here since the Burschenschaft, which aspired to a pan-Germanism superior to that of the German confederation, was disbanded. This region of Europe is a mess; some want Prussian unity at all costs, others seek a greater Germany that can stop the Austrian Empire in its tracks. These are the consequences of the German Holy Roman Empire in 1805, together with the new scenario after the Napoleonic wars and the Vienna Treaty of '15. We are all adapting to a bigger board, and we don't know what game we're playing or if the others seated at the table are allies or rivals. Since 1818 there has been talk in Berlin of some kind of commercial and customs union; if it encompasses other Germanic states then all the better. Franz has mentioned the name *Zollverein* for such an agreement, which could bring economic wellbeing to Prussia. It would benefit you; producers could export sugar without having to compete with the price of beet in nearby countries, because the foreigners would have to pay to introduce their products.' *Interesting.* 'It's good to have friends in Berlin, it helps you glimpse the future instead of sitting down and waiting for it to crush you.' *It's also good to have friends who have friends in Berlin.* 'Yes, that's right. I'll toast to that!'

Although I had already started to plough my field and plant the seeds gradually, on Hans's recommendation

– since I had to sow and fertilise at the same time and concoct the fertiliser myself, a time-consuming task – I wanted to resolve the issue of the soldiers. Ultimately, I wanted permission to bury them in some communal space, so that I could make use of all the land, free of bodies. Other than the 32 yet to be unearthed, I mean. So, I put on clean clothes and went bright and early to Mayor Altmayer's house, to find out if he had any news of the Prefect's negotiations in the capital. I rang at his door and, instead of being greeted by Utta's scrawny face, Mrs Ulmer opened the door. As soon as she saw me, she noiselessly vanished to one side, the same side from which Altmayer appeared moments later. Mrs Ulmer went into the hall, next to the chimney, and began knitting in silence, looking at us from the corner of her eye while we greeted each other and mentioned the change in weather: the snow had ended and the sun was coming out, though it was still bitterly cold.

I didn't want to talk in Altmayer's house. The mayor was in his element there, invested with authority, and I would be at a disadvantage. I invited him to take a walk, without revealing the purpose behind my visit; two people walking together can have differences in height but not in hierarchy. Altmayer accepted and, after throwing a thick coat over his back, walked with me along the river bank. The vegetation seemed to have saved its astonishing range of colours and tones for the sun; I could only make out strategically and beautifully placed blotches, and I imagined the magnificent panorama of details someone with good sight, like Altmayer, who only used a pince-nez to read, could appreciate. The ice was beginning to give way and in some places the Oder was relatively free of floes, which only remained completely solid in areas under tree shade. *Any news from the Prefect, mayor?* 'No. I'm very sorry this issue is taking so long. It must be arduous for you.' *I can't deny it. Nevertheless, I have begun cultivating in the parts free of graves.* 'I understand and I'm happy about that.' *I wanted your advice on something, Altmayer.* 'Go ahead.' *I've been thinking... I've been weighing up the matter, and a solution has occurred to me a posteriori. I regret it has come so late and I was not able to put it on the table from the outset.* 'Any helpful initiative, however late, will be welcome.' *I hope it will help. It occurred to me...* – I think the vacillation in my voice, elevated to an overly sharp tone, did not help to convince the mayor – *that perhaps those bodies could be buried in the communal zone next to the fortress; it's too rough for planting grain and the scrub that grows there cannot be digested by horses or cows. It is, in effect, a terrible wasteland.* I could see the displeased look on Altmayer's face but continued regardless. *I would do all the work, of course; I would dig up all the corpses and bring them there in my cart; nobody would be bothered and they would soon disappear under the earth. Since no one visits that place, no one would realise the earth has been disturbed, and the shrubs would soon grow again.* 'My grandchildren pick berries there in spring, Redo, and it's where we hold the races and shooting contests after the feast of the Immaculate Conception. I don't know if...' *By then there will be no sign that there are bodies buried beneath it.* 'But they will be there, Redo,' Altamyer said tensely, turning around, his hands on his back and his chest jutting forward, 'we know they're there and more will know, because I'll have to inform many people. I don't even know if it can be done; Stein will have to consult the communal regulations and the Prefect... I can't see it happening, Redo, too complicated, too thorny. The whole town would know that there is an illegal burial ground within our boundaries.' *There already is one, Altmayer, on my land.* 'Yes, but now... now it's *your* problem. If we move the bodies there, it's everyone's problem.' I understood him, of course, but suspected no one understood me. I snorted in annoyance, lost for words. 'Don't despair, Redo. I'm sure we'll find a solution. The Prefect is investigating whether there are any antecedents. The legislation on free cultivable land is very recent, as you know, and there are barely any cases we can turn to for reference. What's happening in your field has taken us all by surprise.' *I only ask that you understand how frustrating this juncture is for me. I legally obtained free land, not a cemetery.* 'You're right. That's why we will solve the problem, one way or another.' I understood that there was not much sense in enraging Altmayer. He was the greatest local authority, at least technically. It wouldn't help to have him as an enemy. So I changed the subject and we had a pleasant walk, talking about the good prospects of Baron Geoffmann's next hop and barley harvest.

That night I was rather taciturn and, after spending time in the tavern with Hans, I walked him home in a state of complete sobriety, for which his wife would be grateful; then, instead of returning home, less and less a cabin and more and more a little house because of the work I was doing on it day by day and brick by brick, I took a long walk to clarify my thoughts. I chose a path I had never taken before, which branches off from the river and leads into nearby thickets. The moon was shining bright and, despite the tremendous cold, walking, done at a good pace to warm myself up, was pleasant. Every fifty paces I had a different thought, ranging from Jakob's lessons to the beet to be planted the following day; from the painful memory of Odra to the future, which seemed as murky as the wood I was walking through; from the lewd jokes of the men in Wreech's tavern to the cheese I was making. Serious thoughts mixed in with trivial ones and the lighter weights occupied the same space in my brain as the heavier ones, taking turns to glide past the skylight of my attention. Regina, the tiny, sensible part of me, was nowhere to be seen; she must have been resting in one of my hidden cavities.

I walked and walked without thinking, *pace*-ified. Minutes or quarters of an hour or whole hours later, my meanderings took me to a well-trodden grass path, with tracks from cartwheels and the hooves of horses and oxen; on one of its borders, in a small clearing, I made out a small house with a low, red roof, which was strange because peaked roofs were far more common in this region, to avoid snow accumulating. But if the roof was odd then the small construction built on top of it was even more exotic, a tiny house on top of the main house, like a small-scale model. The constructions weren't identical but resembled siblings of different ages and sizes. My body trembled when a woman's voice addressed me, loud and clear: 'How are things, Redo?' Although thanks to the moonlight I could clearly see the two houses, the normal one and its miniature, I couldn't see anyone at all that could be uttering these words, though I recognised their speaker's voice. *Ilse? Is that you? I can't see you.* A tiny hatch opened in the smaller construction, the one on the roof, and a face as white as the moon above me appeared through it. I had the impression that the witch had somehow guessed it was me, unless the hatch had holes through which the outside could be observed. 'You have come here at this hour because you are anguished by present, future or past.' *All three, in fact.* 'Is there anything you want to know in particular?' *No, you already know that I prefer to wait for things to happen, time passes quicker that way.* 'You're right there, it's annoying to know for certain, as I do, that nothing interesting will happen here until next Thursday.' I preferred not to enquire into this matter. Instead, I asked a more predictable question. *If you don't mind my asking, what are you doing up there?* 'You aren't suggesting I sleep on the floor? It's full of demons. You should know that better than anyone.' *But they don't bite, they're frozen.* 'Yours are,' she added enigmatically. I didn't wish to hear more about this topic either. *Ilse, there's something I've just thought of that I'd like to ask you. Duisdorf, my field's previous owner, you know who I mean, since everyone knew him though no one wants to talk about him... Did he put the bodies there? Did he know they were buried there?* Ilse stayed silent for a long time, as if attempting to align the compass of her mind with some galaxy that the rest of us could not make out in the sky. 'He didn't put them there. But he sought them out. He didn't stop until he got hold of that cursed land, precisely because it was cursed.' *He knew something beforehand.* 'He saw. He didn't see like I do, but he glimpsed something. He was myopic to total reality, just as you are to lesser reality.' *What is total reality?* 'My reality, formed of the part which can be seen, which is yours, and the part that cannot be seen.' *I understand.* 'I doubt it.' *You're right, I don't understand a word, because I don't believe anything exists beyond earth and flesh.* 'In that case, can you tell me what's happening in your field? Those frozen bodies, from other places, other eras, what's your rational explanation? The temperature has changed, it's pleasant in the sun during the day now. Why don't the corpses soften?' *I don't know, some chemical process. Just because we can't describe it doesn't mean it doesn't exist. No one believed in the magnetism of some metals until there were magnets.* 'You're singular, Redo. Besides your secret, which only you and I know in this town, it's strange how someone with so little vision of the real and of the other can be at the same time so intelligent and destined for success.' *I told you not to say anything about the future.* 'You need some encouragement today.' I didn't know how to respond. Something deep inside me, perhaps a sleepy Francis huddled up between two bones, told me she was right. 'Things will work out in the long term. Go home and sleep. You need to recompose, you're not as hardy as the local peasants.' *I'm like the vine,* I countered, *which, though it seems dead from the outside, keeps bearing fruit.* I turned to take the way back. I heard the hatch closing behind me. After a few steps, I expanded my lungs to shout *thank you.* At the very same instant, without even a fraction of a second passing, Ilse's shouted reply could be heard from within: 'You're welcome.'

Damned witch.

During the lessons disguised as dictations it was not uncommon for Jakob to compose his own texts in front of

me, while I copied some passage from the history or philosophy books he supplied, hoping I might learn to think
while simultaneously polishing my grammar and syntax.
We ended up being an inseparable part of the tavern's
landscape: the two of us there at the back, to the left by
the window, one facing the other, surrounded by papers
and books. After a certain number of these meetings no
one paid us much attention and we went unnoticed. But
my eyes were wide open, and I noticed everything. On
one of our first days of joint work, I remember copying a
sentence from Goethe, in which he says the poet is 'like
the eagle, which flies, its gaze free, over different lands,
caring not if the hare upon which it swoops is running
in Prussia or Saxony,' and looking up at Jakob, who was
writing an entry in his diary. He looked tense, a thousand
pouts and grimaces flickering on his face as he moved
his quill, his lips even lightly moving so that he appeared
to be *talking;* looking at him, one had the impression
that language was processed by both the hand and the
mouth. Perhaps I perform the same motions now, like an
apprentice musician humming the notes that come from
the clavichord as they play. I focused on Jakob's face before going back to contemplating the other parishioners
in Wreech's tavern, and saw identical grimaces on their
faces when they spoke. Whoever uses language does it
with their whole face. However, I did see a couple of peasants drinking alone on separate tables, with neutral expressions and distant stares. It gave me the impression
they were remembering. And the lack of expressiveness
on their faces made me think that perhaps they were not
using the part of the brain closest to the face, the frontal

part of the head, but a deeper, more hidden one, the place where – I imagine – my small, contradictory personalities are hidden, where primitive Francis and Peter fight against reasonable Regina. I wondered if the functioning of the brain followed a zonal, geographical logic, in the same way that countries have their centres, capitals and peripheries, all important for the governing of the whole nation. Then Jakob made a very amusing expression, one of unexpected surprise, and my thoughts were interrupted by trying not to laugh.

Three years later, I remember Jakob criticising Benjamin Constant's *Principles of Politics* because, to his mind, 'beneath an apparent denunciation of monarchic despotism hides a bourgeois economic despotism.' *But you are a bourgeois, Jakob.* 'Yes, but not that bourgeois.' We chuckled at these colloquiums, which we began holding in more discreet locations, and when we did go to the tavern we mumbled instead of speaking out loud. That afternoon, three years after the one I am talking of, we were drinking coffee in his beautiful house, full of books everywhere, like an antiquarian bookseller. At the time Jakob was more favourably disposed to the line expressed by Wilhelm von Humboldt in his *On the Limits of State Action*, which never had any practical effect. 'The country is trapped by all sorts of forces looking to the past rather than the future: legal ideas based on the *spirit of the people* or *volkgeist* from the jurist Savigny; Hegel's *Philosophy of Right*, so suspect with its motto that "the real is rational"; the rancid *Weltanshauung* from the heirs of *Sturm und Drang* and their poetic tempests, romantics one day and classicists the next, like Goethe; political theory, which aligns itself with Haller's *Restoration of Political Science* and the absolutist determination of the monarch... There is nobody with any influence in the country who is not working towards the most extreme regression, or for the creation of a dominant greater Prussia. Just you watch, we'll end up with an emperor like the French.' *I'm glad it's you saying this, I'd be more worried if the witch Ilse said it.* 'She claims to traverse the future the way I move through the past.' *I, on the other hand, have finally managed to move only in the present, which is a blessing.* Jakob unhurriedly lit a pipe and sat there smoking it and looking pensively out through the window. To my surprise, since he was not at all given to confidences, Jakob then wanted to share with me a piece of reasoning that I will try to reproduce as best I can: 'I always felt that to live was to be constantly climbing a leafy tree, one's progress impeded by thick branches. A vertical forest. You climb and climb, my parents told me as a child, getting scratches on your legs, cuts on your hands, grazes and bruises all over your body, yet, still, you ascend. One hopes that, at some point, there will be a clearing in the greenery and the sun will be seen, like when mountaineers, so some have told me, scale a peak and see the sea of clouds beneath their feet and above them only the clear sky. I always thought my existence would be like that. We have always been told we must place hope in the future, that the best is ahead of us, that there is always space for what is yet to come. But I am reaching the desolate certainty that it is not so. I've climbed the tree of life and received a blow to the head: when it ends there is only a rocky roof, because we live in a cave; not Plato's cave but one that is less deceptive and terrible because there is no outside. There is no world, no sky, only the cave. To live is to grow enough for your head to hit the top part, until you feel the blood spout. I've felt like I'm at that stage for a while now; huddled up at the top of the tree, squeezed against the roof, unable to move any further without harming myself; with nothing to do ahead of me, no expectations, no desire for change, since I believe that any change can only be for the worse.' *You surprise me, Jakob,* I replied; *I thought you led a happy and comfortable life as a historian.* He made a hand gesture, as if something wasn't worth the effort; perhaps answering the question or maybe life itself. *I don't agree with you, and hope that what's happening to you, this sorrow you are experiencing, will be but a passing inconvenience. The opposite happened with me; for a good part of my adventure I lived squashed against the ceiling, or perhaps against the floor, with the oppression you feel now, but I discovered that, if you hit hard enough, the wall breaks and you emerge into the surface of existence. Sometimes there is sunlight on that surface and at other times it mists over and rains, naturally, but there is always life. I'm not going to go into the subject of happiness, because I believe it's a myth, like Plato's cave, but I do believe there is hope, and occasional fullness and joy. If Odra hadn't died I would be happy, or perhaps I wouldn't: perhaps with time our pleasure would have solidified into routine and joy would have become boredom. Who knows. But even without her, there are still days when I look at the sun shining on my cultivated field and hear the murmur of the river and feel the plants caressing me and see the infinite green surrounding us and, in spite of it all – in spite of the frozen death staring me in the face, or perhaps because of it, because of its constant threat – I feel full and joyful, and I miss Odra and perhaps I shed a tear, of sorrow, or of joy, or of gratitude for the luck of having been able to love her for some time at least and knowing what love tastes like, just as I now know what freedom tastes like. I know my life is good because I do not want to exchange it for anyone else's. I've worked hard to build it, raise it, sow it, give it shape. It's not perfect, but I can navigate it.* Anyone else would have been saddened by the gulf between two utterly different ways of confronting existence, but Jakob showed signs of his infinite bonhomie and unique character: he looked at me affectionately and I know that he was truly happy for me in his heart. And he too felt better for it, unburdened of some of the weight he carried because I, his friend, was well.

His disappearance left a hole in Szonden, like that of Doctor Johnson in Boswell's account, which could not only not be filled but which nobody attempted to fill. No one in these parts is interested in being wise, noble, great.

Including, I must acknowledge, myself; to be like him would oblige me to open myself up more to others, something my circumstances do not permit me to do. In any case, this world is in such bad shape that anyone who does not actively seek ill to others is doing an enormous good.

Andrea Böhm is worried. She doesn't know what's going to happen very soon, when the disease finishes her off for good. We're in the main room of the old building, the green room, and she is looking at us from a large armchair where she is sprawled out, breathing with perceptible fatigue. Alexia, Odra and I are spread around the room on different armchairs; the Vienna light enters, it's midday on Monday, an especially bad time for business. Viennese society strolls outside, tripping over their ostentatiously long dresses. Nothing remains of the weekend's interminable racket. The other girls, Monika, Sophie and Elise, are asleep in the upstairs rooms, exhausted from working until dawn. Andrea, my mother, looks at us. Odra stares out of the window, her hair gathered into a ponytail with hairpins, displaying her exquisite, perfect head; her neck opening harmoniously from its base and her little eyes allowing space for her cheeks and the profile of her fleshy lips. I'm lost in a daydream as I admire her; Odra is gazing out onto the street, Alexia knits, Vienna is drowning in things unsaid. Andrea is anguished, thinking about how we're going to survive without her, who will run the business with her fortitude and energy. She has hired a teacher to instruct me in notions of mathematics and accounting, but it's not enough. The problem isn't the knowledge, everyone knows how brothels and the human soul work, both realities sharing a common ground of desire. The issue is one of character. Odra has character, too much of it, my mother thinks or I imagine she thinks, because at that moment I only have eyes for my haggard Spaniard. I have ideas, ambition, but lack her mettle. And then there's my peculiarity, which she understands, tolerates and even respects but still acknowledges could bring serious complications to running the house. Andrea thinks and thinks, speculates, mulls things over, lucubrates, wracks her brains, because she wants to leave the business to me and not to someone outside the family. Suddenly she sits up with a jolt and the blanket covering her falls to her thighs. We look at her in surprise. *What is it, mother? Are you all right?* 'Of course I'm all right. Alexia, answer me.' 'Speak, madam.' 'You were an actress, yes?' 'Yes, madam, for several years, it was good work but as I'm so short I only ever got parts as girls or dwarves.' 'Then you know how to disguise someone, you know how to do your hair, put on make-up, turn one person into another.' 'Well... to be honest, madam, yes, I do.' And Andrea's eyes open wide.

No one dared to tell me in person, not even Jakob, so the Prefect chose to send me a letter. Three weeks after my arrival in Szonden, as I was ploughing, a government messenger handed me a piece of folded, sealed paper. It had just rained and I was surveying the puddles dotted across my land, wondering how long they would take to freeze; in any case, the spectacle was magnificent. Occasionally, especially while walking, I'd simply behold the enormous size of the world, the unbelievable immensity of the open countryside. For an urban being like me, whose eyes had grown accustomed to the horizon being no bigger than the widest square in Vienna, to now be confronted with those endless distances, which I could not even fully take in because of my myopia, was like launching a bird that had spent its whole life in a cage into the open air or throwing a fish that had always been in an aquarium into a river. I could never come to terms with that open, endless infinitude, which opened out up to the blurry line between the greenness of the earth and the Germanic blue of the sky. From the diffuse horizon came a figure, then a person, then a man, a messenger from less far off and up close just a tired boy. As my hands were covered in frozen mud, I asked him to open the Prefect's card and leave it unfolded on the ox's yoke. He did that and left with a timid salute. The news was dire: the authorities had not come to an agreement about what decision to take regarding the corpses on my land. The case had been added to a dossier to be resolved at one of the next Ministers' Councils, although, the Prefect added, the big load of pending bureaucracy could delay the final ruling by two or three months. I would have liked to let out a piercing cry of rage, but the messenger was still mounting his horse and might have been shocked by my howls. So I grabbed several clumps of earth and threw them with all the violence I was capable of. I could not contain my anger. They were washing their hands of the problem by passing it to a higher authority: Altmayer to the town's council of elders, the council to the Prefect, the Prefect to the council, the council to the minister, the minister to the council of ministers. The matter was grave, especially concerning the sixteen unknown soldiers, bestowed with completely unfamiliar weaponry, but no one knew what to do. Because, ultimately, the land was *mine*, and mine only. As were those dead bodies resting in it. It was my cursed buried treasure.

I don't know how I made the decision, but suddenly, despite my poor sight, I saw everything in total clarity, as pristine as the thawing water. I walked down to the Oder, blinded by its reflection, and confirmed that its flow was completely unobstructed; there were no longer any ice floes in it, thanks to the weak sun of recent days.

I returned once again to the high part of my land and continued ploughing for the rest of the day. I didn't go to the tavern, despite having arranged a study session with Jakob for that evening; leaving him on his own was no problem, he would quickly put his books aside and drink punch with some local. Jakob was universally loved because he was never a burden to anyone. When the sun had fallen in the sky a little, the surface of my land looked like Odra's combed hair after she emerged from a bath, black lines over a base of ochre soil. Only the house, down and to the left when seen from the high ground, and the crosses by the edges, broke the ordered plain, sown and fertilised, which would bear its fruit in some seventy-four days.

I enjoyed that view for a few minutes. I deserved it. I had gone to enormous efforts to get there. To make this land truly mine.

Now, I was going to *earn it.*

I went to the house with the ox, removed the yoke, took some rope and the spade and equipped the horse. I fastened it to the cart and we went onto the path, circumventing the plot until we reached the side with the crosses. I looked around me. In the distance, the giant Udo was taking one of his habitual walks by the bank of the Oder, slow, alone, unhurried. I waited for his image to disappear completely among the trees on the shore. Then I began to dig.

After two hours I realised this was an immense chore for a single person. And there was only one other person whom I could ask to help. I went to Hans's house, carrying a cheese and a nice chunk of butter for Wiesława, in exchange for stealing her husband for an unexpected task. I couldn't think of a good excuse; I told them I had found an enormous ants' nest which I needed to eliminate immediately. Hans, whom I will never be able to thank enough, accepted despite doubting the veracity of my story. When I told him my plan he showed no objection, requesting only that no one would find out he had helped me. We shook hands to seal this pact of silence.

By nightfall, the two of us were so exhausted that I reattached the ox to the yoke and led it to the more numerous grave pits where the beast, by digging with the plough, removed the earth more quickly. We made a mess but this was no time to be fussy. When we had uncovered all the bodies, the moon and the stars were looking down on us; luckily they gave off enough light that it was not necessary to have a bonfire. I put the ox away again, rewarding it with extra feed. Then we took a long, sturdy plank of wood to use as a slope, and with the help of the ropes and the horse's traction we managed to load the 31 bodies exhumed so far onto the cart. It was hard work because they were still frozen stiff and the transparent ice surrounding them made them heavier still. I wasn't sure what to do with the 32 that remained hidden beneath the already ploughed surface. For a moment, an idea crossed my mind, doubtless arising from Francis, Atticus, Helmet or one of the other oafs moving around inside me: *Now or never.* Thankfully I paid it no attention, and did not remove the rest of the bodies. Nor did I mention their existence to Hans. We put the plank inside the carriage, then went back onto the road again, which was rather difficult because the load meant it weighed so much that the wheels had partially sunk into the mud. Once it was on the sand path, we returned to the field and began covering the holes with the dug earth. I soon realised I was completely spent – burly Hans was managing, he has always shown incredible strength – so I decided to save my energy for the second phase of the plan. I resolved to my inner being that the following day I would rise early to cover the earth.

We went down to the river with the cart, luckily no one came past all night. We had to make two journeys because the load was too bulky for the cart. I looked for the closest place to the stream and lined up the back of the cart so it was facing the river, on the very edge of the bank. Hans took out the plank and placed it into the water, only a foot from the land. While he held it firm, I got up into the cart and began pushing the soldiers one by one down the plank, like a pirate throwing the condemned overboard. The soldiers rolled into the water. Some remained still and others went in deeper and got gathered up by the water's course, which led them gently down the Oder. I got down onto the ground and, using our hands or the spade, we pushed along the bodies that had got stuck before returning to the coach, our feet frozen from the cold water. I took Hans back home, thanking him once I was able to catch my breath. Finally, I returned to my hut, where I fell onto my bed like a dead man. As on every other night, then as much as now, I kissed my middle finger, reached out my hand from the bed and touched the floor, sending the kiss to Odra, who slept ten feet below me.

The following morning, woken by the cockerel, I went out at first light. Despite my tiredness I ran, carrying the spade, to fill in the holes so that no one walking past would notice the crime. I piled up the crosses to one side and, when I had finished and after a good breakfast, I returned with the ox to plough all the land that had been occupied by the tombs. I fertilised the hollows and planted seeds in them, mad with contentment.

The hell appeared to be over. And now the earth was all mine, all of it cultivable.

After eating and before going to the tavern, I went down to the river to see if there was any sign of my nocturnal activity. All appeared calm. Occasionally the Oder would carry along some trunks and branches, and what looked like flags or banners. My poor sight did not allow me to discern their national origin or designs.

No sooner had I walked onto the road than I came across the red-haired Finkhölmer, Altmayer's councillor, and conversed with him. I won't recreate it because I was not at my best. I have never liked the suspicious tone Finkhölmer employs with me, as if I had committed some offence. It just so happened that at that moment he was right.

After bidding him farewell, and as I was ascending the hill into the town, Ilse was waiting for me with her wolf, sitting on a broad stone. 'What you've done is madness. Yesterday I dreamt that the river was dyed with blood, so I went down to look before dawn and saw the bodies floating past.' *Everything has its limits, Ilse.* 'The bodies must rest under the earth, between us and the demons.' *I completely agree. But not on my land. In the delta, beyond*

118

Kostrzyn, they will find their place. 'This won't finish you off, but it won't work in your favour. You must control your anger, Redo.' Her eyes seemed redder still because of her rage. She gave me pause for thought. Odra always used to say I was as temperamental as her, if not more so; the only difference was, I needed more stimuli to display it, and by the time it was provoked it had acquired so much energy over so much time that it was quite fearsome. *Thank you, old woman. I'll heed your words henceforth, I believe you wish me no evil and that your advice is guided by good intentions.* 'It is. We must help one another, for as I told you, when night falls, we are alone.' She was right there too. I said goodbye and left her sitting there. Delto approached me from behind, without me realising, and licked my hand. I turned, crouched and stroked the wolf's head. There was something in the depths of his black eyes that reminded me of a cold fire, like flaming icicles.

A cheerful Jakob was waiting for me in the tavern. I apologised for my absence the day before and, although he had not brought any books, we chatted for a while and my curiosity was piqued. He told me he wanted to lend me a volume to read at home at night. I agreed and requested difficult books that I would not fully understand, for what was the use in wasting time with ones that were readily understood. Jakob told me he had become a teacher with only one pupil, but that I was the best possible one. I said I was also his worst, most disastrous pupil and we laughed, as always.

After spending a pleasant night in the tavern, I went home. On the new table, which I had made from some planks, were waiting the numerous papers Baron Geoff-mann had sent to me, his monthly accounts for me to go over. His objective according to his *Meier,* who brought them to me in a fine leather folder, was for there to be no discrepancy between what the tenant farmers on the baron's land produced and what they paid him. My first payment for this accounting work was nothing to sniff at: in exchange for my labour the baron lent me the cow, which was a huge benefit to me, since I could not imagine living without the daily supply of milk and the cheese I obtained thanks to the animal. So I went to great pains to go over the figures by candlelight. I noticed a certain gap between the records and what the baron had been paid, but I felt it was a trivial amount, surely owing to the farmers' struggles to keep their families afloat. I felt that the baron's constant stream of lucre was of little impor-tance but, to compensate him without harming my own peers, I thought of a system of teamwork that might be more profitable and effective for all, landowner and ten-ants. It would eliminate the need for fallow periods and increase the profits. I put it in writing as best I could and added it to the papers I had gone over.

Satisfied with my work and still delighted by my transportation of the corpses to the river, I felt a sense of euphoria which quickly became tinged with sadness when I thought of how much Odra would have liked to share these experiences with me. Looking down at the ground, I drank a skein of wine to her health, to old times in France, and cried, sometimes from despair and other times from solace, until I fell helplessly onto the mattress.

The following morning, after being woken by the cockerel, I opened the door to check the weather only to see two soldiers, their guns slung over their backs, standing to attention while waiting for me. At least these ones were alive.

'You need to come with us.'

If this had been Austria, I would have asked them their motive and we would have discussed the matter, but I was in Prussia and did not know the consequences of opposing authority here. So, without a word, I took my coat and followed them. They escorted me in silence to a covered cart, like mine, sat in the front and invited me to make myself comfortable on the hard floor of the interior. They took the path parallel to the Oder for two or three leagues, until we were some distance beyond the baron's lands. And yet there was the baron, by the river, next to Altmayer, Finkhölmer, Stein and the Prefect of Oderbruch, Hammersköhl, whom I had not met until then. No one shook my hand or said anything, they were all very serious. Hammersköhl simply said the same thing the soldiers had done, to come with them. We crossed a small oak grove and reached some thickets which the soldiers had to clear with long poles. Then we reached a clearing, right by the stream; there, in a bend of the Oder, was a nightmarish reservoir; caught between carefully braided trunks and branches were all the frozen bodies from my land, forming a lugubrious dam, stemming part of the river and sending the waves upwards in an unnatural direction. The bodies were not laid out haphazardly; they were carefully placed in a horizontal position, alternating with soft branches tied to each other and to the trunks, a highly praiseworthy building strategy. I did not understand who could have carried out this act of aquatic engineering, but my problem was that I had not formulated the question properly: it was not who but *what*.

'The beavers could never have imagined coming across such a versatile building material,' Hammersköhl commented, his tone bitterly ironic. 'Light in the water but of a very tough consistency, a frozen body is like manna from heaven to these furry architects. With this wall they can stop the water and fish to their hearts' content in the stagnant pool. A shepherd discovered it yesterday and informed us.' They all looked at me with grave expressions. But I noticed that no one knew quite what to do, beyond being angry. The situation was beginning to become unsustainable and irritating to all concerned, but I was still the most irritated.

Gentlemen, I understand your anger but, if it were up to me, if it were in my hands, you must know that I would go right now to buy some dynamite and blow all these cursed corpses into smithereens, into pieces so small that even the tiniest fish could eat them. I noticed the looks of horror on several of their faces, which was precisely what I wanted to provoke. I had to get it across to them that I was sick of the matter and that that was why I had made the decision, a decision which now turned out to have been wrong, because natural circumstances had intervened. *Before you say anything, I know that all of you have thought to yourselves at some point this morning: 'If only those demonic rodents had not fished the floating bodies and kept them here, by tomorrow morning they would almost have reached the Swedish coast.' That we find ourselves in this place and in this situation is pure bad luck, especially for me. Because I'm discovering these bodies for the second time; they are back to torment me, like ghosts. But I don't believe in ghosts, gentlemen. I believe in actions and their consequences. And now I would like to know if you plan to punish me in some way; if not, I will return with my horse and cart and, with some work, we will take these bodies back to my farm and await instructions from Berlin. If you will allow me to speak freely, gentlemen, the effort and the wait are no small punishment in themselves.*

Hammersköhl spoke, as the highest authority. 'Mr Haupsthammer, we understand your anger. But we must examine the soldiers, especially those whose origin we do not know, and besides, you must understand that you have contravened an order...' *Sorry, Prefect, but I do not agree,* I interrupted, to everyone's surprise. *I agreed with these gentlemen that I would receive the authorities' recommendation. At no point was any 'order' mentioned. I, voluntarily and in good faith, showed conformity in doing nothing until I had received the suggestions from the Szonden council to reach a solution that was acceptable and satisfactory to all. But the local council, most of it present here, has not only resolved nothing, but handed the whole case to yourself, and you, far from resolving it, dodged it like a Spanish matador, letting it continue on its way to Berlin.* 'Mr Hauptshammer,' the Prefect interrupted, but I was sick of hearing him. *There are two incontrovertible facts here: no one has kept their word, which means I cannot be reproached for the same offence; and secondly, and most importantly, you can't punish me for what I do with these bodies because they are* mine, *gentlemen, they are my exclusive property. Isn't Prussia's motto* suum cuique, *to each their own? Well, they were on my land, I am a free owner and since these soldiers are not Christians or cannot be proven so, they will not go to a sacred burial ground. Therefore, they are as much mine as the Prussian land that surrounds them.*

Yes, my mother would have been proud of me. I had mettle after all.

They were all dumbfounded by this unforeseen twist in the tenor of events. Suddenly, the matter had spilled over from the religious sphere to take a dominant place in the controversial geography of justice, that land of borders as murky and open to interpretation as the coast of Scotland. Now we were discussing nothing less than a matter that was sacred in Prussia: the right of ownership and its extension. *Thus, gentlemen, if you have nothing further to add, I will go and fetch my cart to collect what belongs to me. The river's channel is communal, as far as I understand, so no landowner, except me, has suffered any hindrance from this act. I will shortly come back to collect what is mine. A good day to you all, gentlemen.* And I walked away. Among the whispering voices behind me I could hear that of Baron Geoffman, whose accounting books were resting on the table in my room, saying to the Prefect: 'He may be right. Nothing can be done until the problem is cleared up, legally speaking.' And in this simple way, half determination and ingenuity, half good luck, I was spared time in Lebus jail.

The news had already spread across the whole town, reaching the most unexpected places such as the ears of Johanna, the baron's daughter. When she found out from a servant at breakfast that I was returning home to get a cart to gather the bodies from the river, she blushed and said to her housekeeper, Mrs Wolff: 'Tell Emil to prepare the present my father gave me for my most recent birthday.'

I, meanwhile, could not be in a worse mood. I came back swiftly to saddle the horse and gather the ropes and other instruments I thought I might need. I foresaw that the work of untying thirty-one bodies from a fence located in the water would be exhausting, especially when I couldn't even swim. I wasn't sure how I was going to achieve this. I was also afraid of spoiling the friendly welcome I had received in Szonden. My good credit might have run out. So many precautions taken so that my past would not give me away and in the end it was the present that had forced me to march off the chess board. It did me no good to be at odds with the local authorities. The issue was beginning to flare up, and although I had come out of the opening gambit in one piece, it was obvious that the region's leaders were inflexible on this issue. My rhetorical outing by the river could be seen as an act of defiance. And I was under no illusion, they could find the exact juridical means to turn my extractive operation into a general health problem, an assault on decorum, an insult to authority, a public scandal, etc. For years in Vienna we had to deal with the police in order to keep the business open; at times their agents tried to close it using the most outlandish excuses, meaning that I knew well how such things worked. In this case the solution we used to reach at the brothel, that of offering services to the police free of charge in exchange for showing some flexibility, would not be possible. So, as I left the house on my horse and cart, the future did not look clear at all in the medium or short term, since I did not even know if I would be capable of recuperating the bodies from the dam erected by the beavers. I preferred not to mention any of this to Hans, having already placed him at more risk than was necessary.

How quickly the tables turn, I thought. Just the previous night the future had seemed brighter and I had enjoyed a brief moment of joy, believing that I had solved the problem of the soldiers and thinking my luck was changing and the path before me straightening. In just a few hours the macabre case had gone back to the beginning and a shadow had been cast over my happy future in Szonden, because I did not know how this mess would be resolved with the authorities, who were working in a field whose rules I was unaware of at the time. I was certain that the sooner I removed the corpses from the river, the less the damage would be – if my actions had caused anyone genuine harm, since I still could not see any victim greater than myself – so I covered the long road to the crook in my cart in good time, grateful that my horse was young and strong.

I was most afflicted by my thoughts when, despite the clear sky and the luminous brightness of the day, I suddenly noticed that both my horse and I were cast under shadows. How was that possible if only two minutes ago there was not a cloud in the sky?

It was then I looked up and saw it. I had to grip on tight to the reins to avoid falling. In the sky an enormous ball, so big it blocked the sun, rose, gracious and light, like an immense soap bubble. I cursed my poor sight which stopped me appreciating the finer details of the colossal figure, the nature of which I could not discern. It seemed still, but it was so big and tall that I found it impossible to work out exactly which part of the field it was suspended over. In its lower part I felt I could make out a tiny light source, or perhaps it was a reflection from the sun. I had never seen anything like it: it wasn't a cloud, nor was it a bird or an animal. I was completely dumbstruck. Only the awareness that I had to get to the river and collect the bodies made me keep going instead of stopping to properly admire the device.

As I approached the precise section of the Oder I realised I was also coming closer to the immense sphere which, upon closer inspection, was shaped more like a pear or an inverted waterskin. I also began to see that a light or flame was indeed emanating from the lower part, and I noticed that several ropes seemed to be holding it down or hanging from it. Two burly-looking men were tying two of the ropes to several nearby trees. A group of people were congregating by the path. Among the different shapes I could make out a lady, perfectly dressed in a green suit; from a distance I could not tell who it was, but when she turned I saw the glint of a necklace with a carat count only attainable to one person in Szonden. *Johanna*, I thought. *What's she doing here?* She greeted me with a radiant smile. 'We've come to help you. My father's men are already dismantling the dyke made by the beavers. Now we're lowering the balloon, which has a very powerful nacelle, down to the shore, and we'll put the bodies in it to be transported.' So that portent was an aerostatic balloon. I had heard an Austrian general mention them at our brothel, but I had never seen one in flight. I didn't know what to say except *thank you, thank you*, again and again, like an imbecile. That word really was a perfect definition of my mental state, since I felt completely overwhelmed by the circumstances. Entertained by the spectacle, the peasants were happy to help, and with so much manpower the burdensome task was resolved in a few hours. Geoffman's employees made a human chain and placed the bodies one by one on the shore, putting them in place using long iron beams with spikes at their tips; in the clearing another group of people, including myself, was waiting for them, eager to help. We loaded them onto the nacelle, reserving the central cylinder for the flame that heated the air from inside the balloon. Twenty-four standing bodies fitted inside it. The seven remaining corpses were transported by several men, covered in blankets so as not to freeze our hands, and loaded onto my cart. The next steps, according to Johanna, required some care. First, the fire in the inner zinc cylinder of the nacelle was increased so that the balloon could rise with full force; then the enormous fastening ropes were tied to two carts brought along for that purpose, together with mine. In this way, guided along by the carts, the balloon moved across a good part of the Oderbruch, fascinating all the inhabitants who contemplated it, regardless of age. It was a day of celebration, especially for the children, since Johanna had not used her birthday present until then.

'It was a whim, I can't deny it,' she told me, as she travelled alongside me in the driver's seat. 'I found out that Abraham Hopman, the first man to fly over Amsterdam in a balloon, was retiring from his hobby after taking a fright, and I asked my father to give me his airship as an eighteenth birthday present last year. Aerial navigation is a very dangerous activity, and I'm still not sure if I will go up in the nacelle, although those who have flown in a balloon say that it's a tremendous experience, unrepeatable, like seeing the world as if you were a minor god.' Every now and then we turned around to admire the immense fabric sphere above our heads, decorated with animal and floral motifs. Johanna's face displayed an almost childlike look of pure joy, along with unsettling beauty. At a certain moment, contemplating the pearly perfection of her face and admiring the nobility of its interior, I wondered what would have happened if I had not met Odra; I meditated on what would have happened had I arrived in Szonden through a succession of coincidences without the open wound of a recently lost love. Although I acted as if I didn't realise, I was perfectly aware that Johanna was not acting purely out of philanthropy. She had taken advantage of an unforeseen opportunity to help me, impress me, publicly seduce me, having seen that she could not achieve it in private at her father's house. Once I could make out Hans's farm in the distance and, a little further on, the beginning of my plot, a vivid feeling of joy and gratitude ran through my whole being. Whatever the motive, Johanna's help had been lifesaving, providential. *Johanna, I really don't know how I will ever repay you for all you've done for me today. Without you, I think the task would have been impossible.* She looked down with studied embarrassment and then turned towards me, her green eyes close to mine. 'I can think of one way,' she said softly. I didn't know how to escape the situation, so I bought some time. *Do you know the fountain by the abandoned fortress, the one in a clearing surrounded by* trees?' 'Of course.' *I'll wait for you there tomorrow at six in the evening. We'll talk then.* Johanna smiled happily, believing I would declare my love, and I began thinking about how to escape her designs without harming her. I remembered my mother's bitter words regarding Odra: 'Be careful with excessively beautiful people and remember the story of Echo and Narcissus: your fate will always be the echo of your beauty, not its possessor.' In this case, that augury consoled me: Johanna was too beautiful and young to keep her attention on one person for very long. There was another thing in my favour, which I would discover years later: rich people don't fall in love with you, they simply take a fancy to you.

We arrived at my field and together all pulled down on the ropes to lower the balloon to earth, no easy task. Once it was at a certain height, one of the baron's men threw a couple of buckets of water onto the flame in the nacelle and the moment it went out the balloon began to deflate, slowly falling to the ground. When they stretched it out completely to fold it up, I was able to comprehend the immense size of the fabric. We cleared the area of children so they would not see what was to come. Between us we unloaded the bodies, which I piled up next to my cabin, and I effusively thanked and greeted everyone who had helped me. Johanna shot me a complicit smile, reminding me of our meeting the following day. I used the opportunity to hand her the folder with her father's accounts, along with my project to improve the running of his fields.

When I was alone, I went back to contemplating the bodies. They were still intact, frozen, unchanged for who knows how many generations. My problem was still visible to all but at least it took up less space now. As the soldiers neither thawed nor gave off a bad smell, I could leave them there until I decided what to do. Behind me I heard the voice of Mayor Altmayer, who came on foot, accompanied by Jakob. 'What a good afternoon it's turned out to be. It seems that situation has been resolved rapidly and positively. The bodies have come home and the river is once again flowing as it should. And all in a few hours, thanks to the help of Baron von Geoffmann.' Jakob interrupted: 'I suppose, Altmayer, you mean thanks to the help of Baron von Geoffmann's daughter.' They both smiled and gave me knowing looks. *Let it be known that I did not seek her intervention*, I said. 'Of course,' they both replied in unison. 'It is rumoured,' Altmayer added, 'that the younger boys in the region are starting to let their beards grow like yours, to see the results. Your name is in the mouth of all the town's young women.' *It's because I'm n...* 'New and different, yes; tell someone else, Redo,' Jakob commented, and the three of us laughed freely.

A scene has come to me out of the blue, one which took place several days later, in the same place although without Altmayer; Jakob had come to give me a book by Kant, the one he dedicates to perpetual peace, one of the few by the beacon of Königsberg that I can understand, although I do still read the others to shock myself with the extent of my ignorance. The afternoon was fading, the sun setting on the other side of the Oder. Jakob told me that history is not a collection of wars, as some tend to say, but a collection of military errors. 'It is most interesting to read History from the perspective of the defeated, to consider that they were defeated because their generals didn't play their cards right on the battlefield. History is like a ball game in which we are the ball being kicked,' he added. Then he observed that an owl was taking flight amid the darkness, and he opened his eyes with a vivid tremor on seeing the Hegelian metaphor being acted out. I understood then that rationalists also have their signs, signals and superstitions. They operate with culture the way Ilse does with her spectres.

I've lost my thread with the anecdote about Jakob; these days his memory comes to me all the time, perhaps because of the way writing can resurrect people, and I prefer to continue turning back to see what I was narrating: once you pick up the quill you must keep going until you reach the limit of your powers of concentration. Before my digression I believe I was saying that, on the day of Andrea's death, the only one in the last forty years on which our brothel was closed, we returned mournfully from the cemetery in the rain. My mother's death was no less painful for being predictable, since you always hold onto any hope, however vague or esoteric it may seem, rather than accept that the person you are closest to in the world is going to disappear. This does not mean that your mother is the person you love the most, only that no union will ever equal the one between you. Knowing that you have grown inside her, a strange miracle which you will never be able to repeat with anyone, creates a sensation of wonder, like a fantastical novel: for those of us who never wonder if God exists or not, our mother is God, because she creates life. Thus, I experienced the death of God in myself as I returned from the funeral, and

Odra and the other girls, themselves sobbing, did what they could to console me.

When we reached the old building, I saw it for the first time with new eyes, it was my responsibility now. And, honestly, I wanted something different for my life. That old house was as tired as my future inside it. When the girls, who were very friendly and affectionate with me that day, retired to their rooms, I stayed in the lounge with Odra. She tenderly touched my face without speaking and tried to animate me. I looked at her adoringly. She could do what she liked with me; with my mother gone I was at her mercy, like the dog that depends on his master. And she knew it. Suddenly, I said: *I don't want this life, Odra.* 'I understand. I changed my life too and didn't even keep the name I had before.' What's certain is that I never asked her about any of that, for me she only existed after her arrival at that house, and her name was the one my mother gave her, and that was fine. I noticed she was very reluctant to discuss her past, and since I lack a curious temperament or a taste for gossip, I respected her silence. If she ever wanted to talk about it, I would listen to her. That's all. I think my attitude pleased her: not only did I accept her new existence, it was the only one that mattered to me. *The problem is it won't be easy to change, start again.* 'I don't agree. There's always an opportunity. What we must do is take advantage of it when it comes, be brave enough to take it by the horns and accept it.' *That's what I did with you, so I know how it's done.* We laughed. We kissed. And I stopped crying for a few hours. And the opportunity did come, one year later.

Alexia became the Madame, just as my mother had recommended, since Odra never gained sufficient German and obviously I could not play that role. 'Your place, while you learn to develop the disguise Alexia is preparing for you,' Andrea said ' is behind the scenes, pulling the strings.' I would do the accounts, choose the girls, deal with the doctors, discreetly seek out new clients, keep an eye on the movements of the agents of the law, carry out necessary repairs on the building and do an endless number of big and small tasks. Odra would continue to seduce countless men and a small but well-chosen group of noble women, who wished to realise their fantasies in a completely safe space. These women, who paid the most, had their own access through a side door, via the same staircase used by the tailor, so that they could enter the brothel without being detected, free from reproach. No one, save a very observant architect, could link that small door with its chipped frame to the brothel, which one entered from another street. Once inside, I would lead them to the ground floor, where they would not bump into other clients, since the main reception room was on the mezzanine, and I accommodated them in a warm, pleasant space, conceived for a feminine taste, atmospherically lit with candles and replete with fresh flowers. It had no external windows so that no one could be seen, even by accident. The ladies arranged their dates with cards left underneath that door, using initials and clues written on white cards with no letterhead. If the hour they proposed did not coincide with another pre-arranged date, they would simply wait until the moment came; if the space was occupied, I would send them a card with a fake doctor's letterhead, proposing another date or time for the 'consultation'. They were the best clients in every sense, never causing any problems or complaining. The girls, save the odd one reluctant to have same-sex relations even for money, preferred them.

In a way I preferred them too and yet I also didn't, because they all wanted Odra as a *partenaire*.

One day Magnus Duisdorf, a Prussian traveller, arrived at the house. But I'll tell that story another time.

First, I shall return to where I left off, to my early days in the Oderbruch. The following day, the corpses were still piled up outside my shack. I realised that the swifts, crows and sparrows I had to continually scare away so that they would not nibble at the recently planted seeds or the little beet shoots that were beginning to emerge, would not come near the area where the bodies were. To make up for that absence, several people from Szonden and some nearby settlements were now taking walks along the river which, by chance, included a stop next to my land, to see the frozen bodies from afar and spend hours coming up with wild theories about them. Some even asked my permission to see them up close. I refused, since the soil was only recently cultivated and I didn't want them to ruin my work. I spent my time on maintenance, keeping the birds away by cracking a whip Hans had lent me and tending to my animals, although one thought would not stop pinging around in my head; what I was going to say to Johanna that afternoon. I only saw one possible solution, a highly risky one.

The agreed time arrived inexorably. With a grave expression I undertook the long walk to the meeting place. I was dressed as always, with the single variation of a clean shirt beneath my jacket and thick coat. Johanna had adorned herself discreetly but radiantly, with a white dress finished off with an elegant shawl, some singular jewels – among them a rare, fabulous amethyst – and her most dazzling smile on display. Her cheeks were red, her dark locks tumbled down onto her shoulders and her eyes were greener than all the trees around us combined. Her beauty was extraordinary, otherworldly. But at no point did I ask myself why I was about to reject her. After reconsidering it along the way, I decided that her hopes could only be definitively frustrated in one, rather dangerous fashion, since it might put everything that had been achieved so far in jeopardy.

By telling the truth.

'Dearest Redo, I'm so nervous, I don't think I've ever been this nervous before.' *Sit down here, Johanna. We need to talk. But before anything else, you must solemnly swear that what I am about to tell you will remain here, between you and me. You can never tell anyone. Never, under any conditions or circumstances, not even if your life is at risk.* Johanna, hearing my words and the circumspect seriousness on my face, clearly understood that it was not love of which we would talk that afternoon. In fact, we were going to discuss the impossibility of love, the reason – and the reason was not Odra, or not just Odra – why we could never love each other, not then, not ever.

I explained as clearly as possible. She couldn't believe it to start with. Then, although I didn't want to go to such extremes, I did what was necessary for her to understand. She asked for proof and I had to give it. She deserved a full explanation. And, as it could not be done any other way, naturally she understood. And she cried because there was indeed nothing to be done, the proof was con-clusive and unanswerable.

Fifteen minutes later Johanna was calm, somewhat sad but convinced and resigned. I had not at any moment entertained or encouraged her infatuation. 'You've put everything at stake, Redo, by telling me the truth.' *Something tells me I can trust you.* She looked at me tenderly, touched my face and, right there, with a chaste kiss, we sealed a lasting friendship that we still maintain to this day. I love her from the heart and my life in Szonden would be deathly boring without her. But there could be nothing more than sincere friendship between us, which is no small thing. I won't deny that some nights, especially once several seasons had passed since Odra's death and I began to overcome my grief, Johanna's face and body, which she had offered me so often at the beginning, would appear to me at night, sometimes in the middle of my dreams and sometimes during feverish insomnia. But those mental and purely imaginary simulacra have been the only contact between our skins.

Magnus Duisdorf. This story begins with his arrival, for good and for ill. How could I have imagined, that distant May morning in Vienna, when a nervous, moustachioed Prussian – so puny, so inconsequential-seeming – called at our door, that this nobody would unleash such a long-lasting storm in my life, that I would now write in what was once his land. My mother had taught me never to trust any client who did not immediately relax upon entering the building, feasting their eyes on the girls. 'When you see someone like that, with their mind elsewhere,' she would warn me, 'they're either looking for someone or running away from them.' From the moment he entered the room, Duisdorf, whom I spied upon from my usual place of supervision – a high stool in the adjoining room which allowed me to observe everyone through a hole in the wall, disguised behind a crack in the lounge curtains – seemed uneasy, distracted, lacking unequivocal signs of desire. I would understand the reason for this soon after. Barely talking to any of the girls, he went up to the window, looked out onto the street, loosened the neck of his shirt... But he had paid me four gold coins, an amount far higher than the usual tariff, without even asking how much our services cost. I accepted his money, of course, we welcomed any extra sum to cover up holes, in the most literal sense of the expression: our poverty frolicked around in rotten armchairs, covered up with golden fabric. As I continued to examine Duisdorf, our servant at the time, Emma, notified me that the police were waiting for me downstairs. When I got there, I encountered two familiar agents, ones that often came to brothel, sometimes for public matters, sometimes private, mostly public matters which then became private after a brief negotiation. In this case they were looking for a foreigner with a sickly complexion and a prominent moustache, recently sighted nearby. Touching the four gold coins in my pocket with the tips of my fingers and thinking that if the Prussian left without having reaped the benefits of his investment I might have to return his money, I claimed not to have seen anyone fitting that description. They bade me farewell, but not until I had asked them if caution was necessary. 'Nothing to worry about. He's a vulgar cheat who owes money to a powerful person. It would be best for him to leave Vienna immediately, rather than let that person find him before we do.' They left. When I turned around, Duisdorf was partially hidden behind the door which gave onto the staircase. He sighed and said: 'Thank you, I saw them arrive from upstairs and could hear the whole conversation.' *I see you have quite a considerable problem.* 'I do, but you should know that I refuse to pay that tinpot marquess, not because I don't have money but because he was the one that cheated me. He's a con-man. Unfortunately, all the witnesses were Austrians and friends of his, and he could not tolerate me cleaning him out like a novice.' I already had sufficient information to get my bearings, being up to scratch was no small part of my job. *Are you referring to Marquess ***?* 'The very same.' *I don't want to alarm you, but three men have died at his hands in duels to my knowledge. He's infallible with the short pistol.* I could see the cold sweat dripping down Duisdorf's brow, the drops disappearing into his thick moustache. *Don't worry. I have a solution, assuming you are a business man.* 'I am! I told you, it's not money I lack! I left my native Prussia to open a business in Italy, where I wish to spend the rest of my days.' *Italy... that suits my plans, should you want to be a part of them.* 'Let's hear them.' *Come upstairs with me, please.*[4]

The rest was simple. A brief negotiation, a rapid deal, in which in the very worst case I neither lost nor gained

---

4 We must recall that in the second chapter, when he narrates his first conversation with Mayor Altmayer, Redo Hauptshammer tells him that it was Odra who helped Duisdorf. (Translator's note)

anything, and an agreement: I would facilitate his safe conduct to Italy in exchange for something valuable, and that valuable object was the property deeds this story started with. Both stories, the real one and the one being told. If Duisdorf's title deeds were authentic and the land to which they corresponded real, I would have the chance to reinvent myself with Odra in another country, where nobody knew us and where we could put my new personality to the test, have a free existence and a future. New place, new names, new life. If the title was false, I would lose nothing except a favour owed to me by a Minister of the Empire for services irregularly rendered. As the minister was given to showing up at our establishment, blinded by Elise's charms, it would not be difficult for me to earn more. Duisdorf left that same night for Italy in an official carriage and Odra and I stayed up most of the night reading the document, savouring its apparent legitimacy and wondering if this truly was our door to beginning again elsewhere.

The only good thing about having enjoyed very few happy moments is that their gold maintains its lustre over time. And though their memory can be bitter, or bittersweet, they are not diluted through the myopic lens of the passing years. They're always there, clearly visible in the memory. When you have lived for long enough, you realise that surviving an incident is more relevant than whether the event itself was positive or negative, because the majority of moments in the majority of years in the majority of a life fade with an ease that's terrible to witness. We are condensed oblivion. Those gold coins are the only thing we will take to the other side, once Charon's tax is deducted; the meaning of everything resides in them.

Thanks to Jakob I now have a culture, which affords me one of civilisation's most precious gifts: to enunciate common names so that they appear different. Culture allows us to present ancient platitudes as if they were new.

The bodies were still there.

People walked past and looked at them. I could detect in their curious expressions the inherited pangs of conscience which every half-buried – or half-unburied – body awakens in people. One day the vice rector came, accompanied by two nuns, and gave me a circular hand gesture which meant: 'I'm on important pastoral business, we shall meet as soon as I am free.'

One afternoon I sat down close to the cold soldiers, turning my back to them and looking towards the Oder. Although I couldn't make out the details, that sight soothed me: above, a blue strip; in the middle a green strip; a thin, blue line – the river – a little further down and then everything green until the beginning of my rustic farm. I found it calming to think that nothing in that landscape would change for decades – and it hasn't.

Around this time I noticed that the birds were wreaking small-scale havoc on my planted beets, thus threatening the prosperity of my harvest. Several plants had peck marks and holes in them and I was worried about the effect this could have on the stalks, that they might attract parasites or diseases in the bulbs. This was the fuse which led me to my final resolution in the case of the dead bodies. The idea was simple and so was the execution. It was an idea associated with a past I had read about in one of Jakob's books, which told the story of the Lange Kerls, the tall boys, also known as the Giants of Potsdam, which Frederick William of Prussia had created as a royal guard in the 18th century. The monarch's intention was to have a personal regiment formed only of boys of proverbial stature, chosen from the best German stock. This same king, in addition, had doubled the Prussian army, a detail which interested me, since I saw in it a sort of natural law impelling the powerful to move pieces in geometric progression and keep history moving. Conquering double the number of towns, multiplying legions or regiments, doubling the length of one's reign compared to the previous leader or doubling the country's territory, like the Mughal Aurangzeb or Alfonso IV the Brave of Portugal, who conquered all the land from the Tagus to the Algarve. Roughly around the time of my arrival in Szonden, Humboldt reached the conclusion, after his American journey, that thanks to the conquest of the New World in the 15th century, 'the works of creation had doubled for the inhabitants of our old Europe.' Universal history as numerical progression. I thought that one way of resisting this mathematical-political madness, this reasoning which is actually unreasoning, was to cut the troops, reduce the size of the hussars. Scare away the birds and reduce the soldiers. The solution, which stemmed from the synthesis of those ideas, took hold of me like a vision. It didn't take long to make it material, accustomed as I already was to digging. Uncommonly so.

And so, without too much thought, everything was resolved. Overnight, 31 scarecrows were placed geometrically across my land. 31 soldiers, upright, buried to their knees, so that the wind did not blow them over. There they remained, impassive, still frozen, independent of the sun and varying temperatures. From any corner of the land it resembled a macabre chessboard, with all the bodies turned towards the east so that the Oder could gather their gazes and carry away their detained horror forever.

I understood the seriousness of what was coming when I saw Hans approaching the boundary, beholding the sinister spectacle, removing his cap and holding it between his hands before turning back towards his land in anguish, shaking his head.

Hours later, Udo stopped by the farm for a moment, beholding this tragic sight from on high. He looked at me. *It's not my war*, I communicated with a shrug of the shoulders.

I needed scarecrows. And I wanted all my land freed up. Arranged like this, between rows of plants, they were no bother. My property deed mentioned half a horseshoe of cultivable land, not a part of it. All the better that I never dug up the 32 bodies still waiting in the gloom; luckily only Ilse and I knew about them. These were the reasons I used to convince myself, but I later understood that I was annoyed with the authorities, who had been incapable of finding a reasonable solution. As if in all the Oderbruch there were no empty spaces, unused, communal or not, or forests, precipices, dried-up irrigation canals or invisible inclines in which, with the slightest intelligence and resolution, the bodies could have been decently buried after a short ceremony.

Besides, there was another motive, which came out in the conversation with Jakob when he headed over to my farm, alarmed by the news that was spreading. 'Have you lost your mind Redo? This... this can't be. I understand your annoyance, but this is too much.' *They're my dead.* 'The dead don't belong to anyone, Redo!' *Anyway, this way I'll force them to find a solution.* 'That's the only reasonable explanation I can find for why you've done this: an act of defiance, putting all your eggs in one basket. But you're risking an overwhelming response.' *They won't let me bury them because they say they need to examine the unknown warriors first, for security. They won't authorise me to get rid of them because they don't know where to put them. Nor will they let me leave them out in the open. Jakob, my dear friend, please can you ask the reasonable Prussian authorities a most simple question: what on earth do they want me to do?* 'You think the only way out is to force the situation, but it would be a shame to throw away the successful start you've made in the town. People are getting nervous. For days now all the children in the region have been prohibited from walking past here. Some old people who have been walking the bank of the Oder since last century are now avoiding this part to avoid seeing the bodies. Then there's the issue of respect; even I, an agnostic, see something terrible and improper here, Redo. How can you walk among these bodies and not be moved?' *Because I believe they are a lesson, Jakob, as a historian you should understand. It's an opportunity, now that we are living in times of peace, for Prussians to see or recall the horrors of war. Just as the sea washes up shipwrecks onto the shore, the earth expels its drowned. Those soldiers are here because they died, that is, because they were killed. The citizens of Szonden are not horrified because they are corpses, but because they are young and recognisable, because their eyes are open and their flesh is still fresh, because it looks like their lives were only recently torn from their bodies. This is what no one wants to see. That war puts their sons in the firing line. That, if there is another war against France or Austria, their sons will be the next corpses. That's why everyone wants to bury them at any cost: no one wants to hear the warning or see the war's predictable results. Those who will be the future recruits, the children, are prohibited from seeing them. Those who would suffer the future losses, their parents, avoid looking at them. Those who will order these losses want them to be invisible. These bodies are the foundations upon which empires are constructed and, like the foundations of a building, someone has decided they should be beneath the earth. If we don't see them, they don't exist. If the horror is invisible, there is no horror. That's all.*

Jakob fell silent in shock.

He put his arms on his waists and turned around to observe the nearest soldier. It was one of the Napoleonic twins. It was looking towards the river in surprise, with the dumbfounded expression of someone who has died before their time and does not understand or cannot accept it. Jakob contemplated it. Through the ice he saw its blushed cheeks, full of life, uncorrupted, terser and younger than his own despite having been dead for years. He squatted first and then sat on the ground, defeated. We said nothing. I also sat down. I also looked at the soldiers. In detail.

I saw the lesson they were teaching me: live now while you have time, don't resign yourself to a lesser life than the one you desire. One day you will be cold like us.

I remember a sentence Rahel wrote in a letter to me, years later: 'Speaking of utopias, did you know that *utopić się* in Polish means *to drown*?'

I've gone back over this piece of writing to check if, in my digressions, I have left out elements I had planned on including, and I have seen that at the end of the third chapter I promised to relate how Odra and I learnt how not to get drunk. I believe that now, after all I have said, it will be better understood. Odra and I had worked out my fictitious personality down to the last millimetre; we took our time, from the final days in Vienna, working on my training, facilitated by the appearance Alexia had designed for me. But it was in France that we perfected my reinvention as Redo. We had to create a citizen with a clean or invisible past who could pass as a farmer-land-owner, no easy task with my childlike Viennese frame. We were certain that there would be critical moments, like private parties or public dances; key events that had to be overcome without arousing suspicion, and an abstemious person always arouses suspicion, especially when they're new in town. Neither did I permit myself the luxury of not attending festivals; *not being present* in society draws just as much attention as being present all the time. No: I would have to socialise and converse with others, I would have to celebrate, I would have to drink in big and small groups and co-exist in a collective for hours, since the final objective used to be – was, will be, is, still is – to go unnoticed, like the insect which, by staying still, avoids detection by the bat, or the rodent that becomes part of the nocturnal landscape in such a mimetic fashion that it does not awaken the owl's attention. I would also have to learn to smoke a pipe. I was easy prey, my only possibility of survival lay in going completely unnoticed. I had to behave like just another local. Luckily, the blonde hair inherited from my Austrian mother and my strong complexion – perhaps inherited from my unknown father – made it easier for me not to stick out too much among all those pale Teutons with fair eyes like mine. There was no other solution. Everything had to be controlled, I had to watch myself to the point of virtue, make self-awareness an artform, with the help of Alexia's disguise.

So Odra and I learnt not to get drunk. We thought it was a good idea not to come straight to Szonden, but to take a long detour before setting up here, to put ourselves to the test outside our element. Like any Spaniard Odra knew the French grape harvest always needs married couples as labour. So we packed our bags, leaving the brothel in the hands of the small but energetic Alexia, and headed to Lyon at the end of August in the last happy year we shared. That journey presented several advantages for us: in the first place, it familiarised me with working in the fields, allowing us to ask a thousand questions about cultivation techniques, harvests, gathering, sowing and tools, equipment, etc. In the second place, because we both worked, our savings increased, essential for when we got to the Oderbruch. In the third place, it helped me strengthen my shoulders, big but underdeveloped and unsuited to physical labour. Fourthly and no less importantly, the foremen gave us free wine, taken from the excess from the previous Beaujolais harvest. This fitted into our plans like a glove.

For four months, between September and December, with special devotion – for we glimpsed on the horizon the possibility of a fully free existence in which we could live together without restrictions for the first time in our lives – we worked hard at gathering the September grapes, treading them and treating them in October so that the liquid could be stored in oak barrels, and we were even hired from November to the end of February for a range of jobs on the farm, thanks to our good command of French, which our work in Vienna had forced us to acquire. I can see now how happy we were in those months, working during the day and breaking our backs drinking *vin de primeur* at night, laughing and making love as our young bodies, free and brimming with desire, cried out at us to do. Thanks to hundreds of refillable leather wine-skins – Odra preferred to use the Spanish word, *botas* – we learnt to observe and control the body's reactions to alcohol, gradually incrementing my resistance and learning to detect signs of inebriation early on, so that ingestion could be stopped in time or spaced out by mixing it with water, a technique taught to us by some beautiful Castilian girls who worked alongside us during the harvest. During the first days, dawn was torture; no sooner had we woken up than we were required to go out onto the fields, half-dazed, to work under the thirty-degree sun, our bodies dying of thirst. On many occasions we would gather the grapes with one hand while with the other we held onto the spiny trunks of the vine so as not to fall. But any sickness would disappear when I saw Odra looking at me in amusement, in a similar state of discomposure, whispering in her clumsy German: 'again, tonight!' All these years later that memory still leaves me breathless. We ate little, to save even more, consuming only the lunch of bread and cheese we were given at midday, which made us even more sensitive to alcohol at night. In the end we achieved our goal and I developed a tolerance similar to that developed by the spy who, little by little, immunes himself to the most lethal poison.

Jakob told me this much later but, roughly speaking, it happened like this: his friend, Councillor Franz Reit-man, the Prefect of Oderbruch, a Berlin Bishop, Pastor Stein, Altmayer, Baron Ernst von Geoffmann and a high ranking officer in the Berlin police met in secret in the Howisch Tower. Situated in the New March, thirty miles from Königsberg, it was a private place, shrouded in leg-end; it is said that the Brothers Grimm used it as the setting for some of their stories. The gentlemen locked themselves away in the tower and reached the conclusion that what was happening on my land went against all laws, human, divine and Prussian. And they made a sug-gestion to Councillor Reitman which he had no option but to approve. My fate had been decided. And although the verdict was overwhelming, years later I recognise that it could have been much worse.

Meanwhile, I continued with my agricultural tasks, fo-cussed at the time on tending to and extending my small private allotment, upon which a part of my daily subsistence depended. As Hans had finished the most arduous part of his hop cultivation, he was able to help me and, above all, advise me. I soon had a small allotment with tomatoes, beans and, above all, potatoes, a key element of the local diet. Hans asked me how much time it had been since I'd had a hog roast or a cut of ox. I answered that I did not even remember those dishes having existed. Apart from the lambs given to me by the baron upon my arrival, I had spent weeks getting by on cheeses, eggs, some vegetables, bread and cow's milk. I had not developed any muscles but my body was fibrous and resistant, strong as it had never been before.

My land had turned into a small festival. While the solution to 'the problem of Redo's field', as the matter was already known, was being prepared, innumerable people would show up at the farm with the most implausible excuses, or without any at all. Only children were prohibited, but otherwise half the entire Oderbruch found a moment during those days to come to Szonden and, specifically, to the now famous farm by the river where they observed the 31 corpses with astonishment, wondering how it was possible that they could remain frozen in the face of the oncoming spring.

On one of those afternoons, Ilse invited me to go to her house to show me something. I went with her, since the experiences she offered were like no others: what Ilse said or did was only possible coming from her mouth or her white hands.

I could never have imagined from the normal, almost beautiful, outwards aspect of her house – except for the little replica house on the roof – just how inconceivable the inside was. She had painted all the walls black, even the ones in the kitchen, using some kind of tar or pigment. She told me that this gloomy atmosphere kept away evil spirits and trolls from nearby mountains. Despite the bizarre level of darkness the house was well lit and even warm, thanks to several oil lamps with crimson screens and red candelabras, which lent it a decadent air. The crimson lighting reminded me of some of the rooms in my Viennese brothel and I could not help feeling at home, despite the horror vacui of the bedrooms, full to the brim with furniture, fabrics, strange tools, books, indecipherable machines, junk rescued from rubbish tips, cabalistic signs painted on the walls, and many other disconcerting visual distractions. But the strangest was yet to come.

Ilse pressed a spring in the form of a book on one of the shelves, revealing its true nature as a door to an adjoining room. It was a small room – I had to crouch – and thanks to some architectonic devilment it formed a space that was indetectable within the house. 'The only way it could be found is by tearing down the whole building.' The walls were red, the only light came from white candles and there was a single piece of furniture occupying almost the entire space: an enormous round table, on top of it innumerable clay figures, about the height of a fist. *What's this?* 'Don't you know?' I expressed my bewilderment. 'It's Szonden,' she replied, 'or rather, it's us, the citizens of Szonden.' I looked more carefully. In the centre of the table there was an isolated figure with quite a lot of space around it. I realised that it was Stein inside his church, the biggest building. That helped me orient myself: the way the people were distributed, basically grouped by families and houses, suddenly made me see the entire town, as if from a bird's eye view. One figure was twice the height of all the rest; I did not have to ask who it was. I searched at one edge and saw Ilse – the only white figure on the board – and me, next to a smaller piece, Delto, the three of us together in our isolated corner. I observed that some effigies had a small piece of blue paper on top. When I mentioned this, she responded: 'Those are the ones who will die this year.' This gave me goosebumps. I checked, and none of them appeared to be of any importance to me.

Then Ilse gave me a very serious expression, her irises emanating fire. 'I'll say this only once; this is your only opportunity. Do you want any of these figures to disappear?' I couldn't believe what I was hearing. Clearly, I didn't believe that Ilse possessed such a power, but something made me wonder what could happen if she really did. I replied: *Of course not. Thank you, Ilse, but no.* And then, somewhat uncomfortably, I asked for permission to leave, solemnly declaring that I would not say a word about what I had seen or heard. She didn't reply. It was as if she expected me to keep silent.

Occasionally Jakob came to distract me, to make the time pass quicker. He thought I didn't notice his elegant way of helping me, but I did. On one of our walks around my farm, whose perimeter we covered in roughly thirty minutes, he told me about a youthful, unreciprocated love. I believe that, in a way, he stayed single for a reason similar to my own, and this experience during his university days had affected that decision.

In the History faculty at Berlin, during the final year, a new student had arrived from Munich. A good-looking, shy Bavarian girl. At that late stage in the course almost all the students sat in groups, always on the same rows in the lecture theatre, following a routine so that they avoided having to think. Jakob, with that whiff of notoriety possessed by more impertinent students, used to sit alone in the front row, where he could pay full, careful attention to the lectures. The Bavarian arrived in mid-October, and because she was nervous and did not know where to go, she also sat in the front row, next to Jakob. They didn't talk at all on the first day, only exchanging occasional, fleeting glances. The girl, Klara, was the only woman on the course. The other lads, who until then had viewed Jakob with indifference, now envied him. But Jakob, who read so passionately about revolutions, was not prepared for an internal, hormonal one. Half his brain tried to concentrate on the lectures on historical reasoning, Caesar's Latin or the Punic wars, while the other half boycotted this discipline and daydreamt about even closer contact with Klara's plump flesh. 'The best thing was,' Jakob confessed, 'the less I did, the better things went: because I was too scared to talk to her, I didn't make a mess of things; because I made no uncouth or invasive movements towards her, I earnt her trust; because I responded to her queries or questions with rigorous exactitude, without giving too long-winded answers, out of pure embarrassment, she did not detect my pretentiousness or my irrepressible pedantry. In short, my inexperience turned me into a master of seduction, a wise Casanova,' Jakob said. I could not help chuckling, and he soon joined me. 'For several reasons, Klara and I spent our days overwhelmed by nerves, both so insecure that we never said anything to each other, instead spending our days in a tempestuous, happy silence, including during times of leisure and rest, since we ate together in silence.' *You can't be serious.* 'Just so. We would sit together early in the morning, walk together during breaks, in silence, and have lunch at the same table, in a nearby inn, facing each other, without even daring to look at one another, our cheeks bright red. It took me a month to say my first non-academic word to her, and six months to give her a chaste kiss on the cheek. I believe they were the happiest weeks of my life.' *It doesn't take a lot to make you happy, my friend,* I added, his deep laughter alarming curious walkers loitering by the river. *So, what happened in the end?* 'Ah,' Jakob answered, melancholically, 'she returned to Munich in June.' *What? That's it?* 'Yes, that's everything. We graduated and agreed to keep up correspondence. In the third letter she told me that her parents had pledged her in marriage to a duke of Thuringia with a promising military future ahead of him and that's where it all ended, to my displeasure.' I was going to follow this with a joke, but I saw that Jakob's face had grown sombre. Until that moment I had never wondered, nor asked, why my friend had never had a wife.

Jakob died in 1849, as sweeping changes and revolutions shook Europe and Prussia to the core, events he followed so avidly that perhaps his heart suffered the consequences.

One morning they came to find me; Dolores, Jakob's housekeeper and the Lebus doctor's helper, mounted on the same horse. 'He's had an angina in the chest, it's very serious, come with us.' I mounted my horse and we left at once. The moment I crossed the threshold, the doctor's expression cleared away any doubt; he didn't need to speak to communicate to me that Jakob was in his death throes. He could barely speak and his breathing was weak. I sat down on the bed, next to him, squeezing his shoulder; I wasn't sure if it made sense to encourage him, but I tried, telling him that he would overcome the cardiac arrest and we would walk together again soon. 'Don't tire yourself out, friend,' he replied slowly, almost syllable by syllable, 'I know I'm on my way out.' I asked the housekeeper, whose eyes were moist, and the two medics to leave me alone with him. They left and, summoning up all my courage, I said *Jakob, my dearest friend, there's something important I must tell you, something I've kept...* He interrupted me with an arm movement and smiled. 'I know,' he said, simply. Then my eyes began to fill with tears. 'I wish only to ask you one thing, Redo,' he whispered, struggling greatly. *Of course, whatever it is, whatever you want.* 'No matter what happens, do not bury me in that cursed field of yours.' We laughed and, amid this laughter, Jakob died, by my side, with a happy look engraved on his face.

The same one I have whenever I remember him.

Let us return to the Oderbruch of those days, the year of the bodies.

The atmosphere was tense, everything seemed to point to the prelude to something. On those nights I could hear Ilse's wolf howling, near the house.

It happened one sullen, electric morning. It was dark outside, the clouds presaging a storm that never actually broke. I was gathering beet leaves to feed the animals. I stood up straight to stretch my back muscles and, under the greyish sky, saw an enormous but silent committee of men, on the path by the Oder. I was just as surprised by their number as I was by that caravan's sonorous discretion. Of all those people only one man, wearing a large hat and immaculately dressed, did not hesitate to cross my land on foot, treading carefully on the unplanted areas. Though I couldn't see him clearly, something told me he was looking me directly in the eye as he slowly approached. Although I did not know him and had never seen him before, I knew who he was when he faced me and held out his hand without introducing himself.

'Redo Haupsthammer, you are welcome to Prussia. We deeply lament what has happened to you. We want you to live in peace. But we also desire peace for others. The children are asking questions. The Pope in Rome is asking questions. The Berlin newspapers are thinking it might be a good idea to send reporters here. You understand it's not convenient for death to cause such commotion in a country that is at peace. For the moment, I mean. One day a great German country will form and a price will have to be paid for that. Perhaps more soldiers will die on these lands for that cause. Perhaps they will be buried here. Perhaps, who knows, you and I will be buried under this dark soil. The future is also written in darkness, illegible until time sheds light on it. Perhaps, together under the earth, we will have an eternal conversation like this one. But I cannot permit this aberration now, Redo. This is your field, that is true, but everything surrounding it belongs to me. Those four paths delimiting your possessions are part of mine. I respect your decision, but I must keep things under control. These bodies provoke nightmares and I must safeguard the Prussian people's sleep. Tomorrow I will send an army of men who will erect a fence around your land, with a wide gate to which only you will have the key. That wooden fence, behind which we will plant trees and shrubs so that, with time, people will not even know there is a fence behind it, will completely close off your property and be two or three heads taller than the tallest men in Oderbruch – and I've heard there's a giant in these parts. Then, when you die, because I know you have no children and do not want a wife...' *I had a wife.* '...So I have heard, and I lament her early death. When you abandon this world, Redo Haupsthammer, the agents of the kingdom of Prussia, on mine or my successor's order, will enter this land and, even if you have left a will, declare it of national interest because it is a danger to the public, and those frozen corpses will be buried so deep, their feet will stick out on the other side of the globe. And we will close the farm forever, alleging that these lands are poisoned.' *They are, Majesty.* 'Not if no one can see them. You are the last person who will ever enjoy this cursed and splendid land, because in a field of death there is also food. Be happy here, Redo; have a prosperous life, take everything that Prussia can freely offer you, and let's rid the generations of this horrible sight. A nation cannot survive with the truth exposed.' *And we are going to bury it in the open.* 'We will bury it in the open, yes. Have a good day, have a good life, citizen Redo Haupsthammer, the man with no fear, the first free farmer in Szonden, the vassal who filled the king of Prussia's boots with mud.'

He shook my hand and left, walking with his head lowered, his hands together behind his back, without avoiding the puddles.

I must bring this to an end, thus it will be necessary to record a number of things.

1. Ilse predicted that one day a word would be invented to define fields like mine, frozen for most of the year: '*permasnow*, or something like that. Your field is a transplanted fragment of the Arctic. The bodies which we know remain beneath it shall be discovered by the beings of the future, just as today we are removing mammoths from glaciers.'
2. I have never heard Mrs Ulmer's voice.
3. Jakob once asked me, contrite and somewhat melancholy: 'Do you think some transient and intense affairs can be better remembered, or more definitively, within the space of a lifetime, than long and presumably

profound relationships, sustained over many years?' After thinking for a while, I answered: *No*.

4. Never, over all these decades, have I managed to meet vice rector Stein on his own; we still walk past one another, and he always laughs and tells me he owes me a courtesy visit to welcome me to Szonden.

5. Hans found it strange that my body became stronger and more defined the year I arrived, but not more muscular. 'How is it possible, Redo, that you have not gained corpulence, after so many hundreds of hours' work.' *I've focussed on acquiring knowledge instead*, I said, to evade the question.

6. I have never again got down on my knees before anything or anyone. Not even to kiss.

7. When I turned sixteen, my mother said: 'It's not good for the business for you to call me "mama" or "mother" in front of the girls, far less the clients. From now on you will call me by my name, Andrea.'

8. Once Udo surprised me without my beard; a hen escaped very early one morning and intuitively I ran after it, without realising that I hadn't prepared myself to venture outdoors. This had never happened before. Unfortunately, on that day, Udo happened to be walking by, on the way to fetch the honey from a beehive. He pointed at me, open-mouthed. 'You've shaved.' And I said yes, I had a skin problem and needed to expose it to the sun. I couldn't leave the house for a week; luckily Alexia had also made a short beard for me. Udo died recently, never having known money.

9. The bodies are still here. In the same position, standing, scaring the birds. Of course, they are still frozen,

as they were on the first day, despite the sun's rigour and the heat of thirty-five summers.

10. Sometimes there are knocks at the gate. I never open it. They might be curious passers-by, or journalists, or unwanted visitors. Those who know me know that they must take the small yellow stone at the foot of the cork tree and throw it in through the fence. I can see it fall from the window where I write or hear it if the earth is dry.

11. The investigations into the 16 soldiers of unknown origin and Germanic physique were carried out with no definitive conclusions. It all came to nothing. Ilse the witch said that they were warriors from another time. As for me, I have never cared who they were or when they came from.

12. Another of the great favours Jakob did for me was helping me discover poetry. It all started on the day he praised the metre of one of Schiller's odes. I asked him what the word *metre* meant. 'Why, the dimensions of a poem, the syllable count, the combinations of metres and strophes, etc.' That made sense to me, I replied. 'Why?' *Because I understand the guiding principle. If poems obey a law they interest me and must necessarily be the best literary works, the essence of the creative.*[5] 'Why should that be so, Redo? You never cease to surprise me.' *Because if you know that you can only deal five blows, the last one is dealt along with the first. It's like sowing*

---

5 Haupsthammer appears to be making an oblique allusion to the similarity between the words *Erdichtung* (invention) and *Dichtung* (poetry). (Translator's note)

trees in a field: you must be quite sure of the end result before planting the first one. Jakob massaged his new beard. *I want to know more, friend; if it's no bother, one day a week we will read poetry and you will explain it to me. I want to know all about this form of measurement.* I am very interested in measurement. In fact, I would say that measuring constitutes my only obsession.

13. Fifteen years ago, I raised a second floor above the southern part of the house, under the advice of an architect from Lebus. I needed space for my library, though I still write in the living room, close to Odra.

14. Ilse did not die, she disappeared. She vanished overnight with her wolf, both of them already very old. Finkhölmer, the new, rubicund mayor, who had been Altmayer's assistant, concluded that Ilse had left Szonden. But I know she hasn't. Sometimes I see her on my land, looking at the soldiers, always sufficiently far away so as not to scare me.

15. I have never wished to unearth the 32 bodies which never came to the surface. After an intense downpour on the 15th April 1839, just to verify my mathematical intuition, I sunk a long, thin iron spade into the soil, in the area which Ilse had pointed out years before as the place where the rest of the macabre host lay. When the iron reached six feet, it hit something hard. Enough. When I pulled it out, the spade had traces of watery, cold blood.

    The body of Odra, another victim of war, is body number 64.

16. I believe that Odra, who always kept her Spanish surname, accepted the name my mother gave her as a way

of erasing the past, just as I gladly accepted mine. A new name is a rebirth, a new life. Although of course I have not forgotten what I used to be called.

17. My nerves are intoxicating me, I think that knowing I am on the brink of finishing this document will give me the courage to tell the truth.

18. Because I know that some of the things I have related are not true. At least not completely.

19. We always knew our plans would be a success because in northern countries people are colder with each other, and physically more distant. 'In Spain, Portugal and Italy,' Odra told me on one of our French nights, 'you'd be discovered in a matter of months.'

20. I have most certainly invented some things: it's difficult for a myope to remember details.

21. Perhaps there's no need to tell the truth. Perhaps we know it already?

22. In 1848 I stopped going to mass for appearance's sake. I've never gone back.

23. I've never been less than ten metres away from Ingeborg the miller; avoiding her and keeping her at arm's length has been one of the hardest jobs I have ever had. Leibniz wrote: 'if we were to magnify the brain until it is the size of a mill and walk around inside it, we would not find consciousness'; Ingeborg's mill proves that, were this enlargement to be realised, we wouldn't find guilt either. That's why I avoided Ingeborg. Her and others who approached me out of error, like Johanna. There has been no shortage of perfumed handkerchiefs or garments to come through this fence, accompanied by written notes from different

women. The poor things, they couldn't even imagine. I keep them carefully; their smell keeps me company on some lonely nights and fires my imagination.

24. It was impossible to work with Johanna's husband, I could see that from the outset. I had known quite a few insolent youths like him in Vienna, all cut from the same cloth: aristocrats and heirs to enormous fortunes they had never fought for. Perhaps they feel destined by royal and natural law, deserving excellence by right. They don't earn, they just take. I hate armies and weapons, especially since I see their traces daily, surrounding my house on all sides, but I recognise one good thing about them: they take idlers like him and impose discipline on them, teaching them that there is something superior to them, taking them down a peg or two. Stay away from the rich man who has never worked or been a soldier, he's a natural tyrant. That is what Johanna's husband is like, a despot who doesn't even value what he has at home and takes advantage of his already preeminent situation to violate any local young girl without consequence. I've never hesitated to mention everything that reaches my ears to Johanna, despite the danger of that despicable Junker challenging me to a duel. 'You think he hides it? You think I haven't seen him rummaging around in the skirts of the servant girls in my own house?' What times we live in, where things like that can happen. On many occasions the idea, half serious and half in jest, has come into my head that I should open a brothel in Szonden, with that swine as its only client. The problem, now I think of it, is that he might

not be the only one. I hadn't considered the far from minor detail that, were I to open a brothel, I would not have to escape to Magdeburg to fulfil my own needs. I know how the business works and am unconcerned about my respectability, and there are no houses of ill repute for many leagues around us.

25. I'm not being serious, I would never repeat that atrocious experience, whereas I'd love to give Johanna's husband another thrashing.

26. Johanna revealed to me some months ago, laughing, that she had once heard gossip among the women who work in her house – she said 'among my servants' – about Jakob and me, for being such good friends, given that we were 'the only men who have not married or had lovers in Szonden'. I had no option other than to laugh with her.

27. I remember the first beet I extracted with my own hands. It was an unforgettable moment, the first time for decades that this land had offered life instead of death. Sowing sugar beet is not easy. To pull them up you have to yoke the ox and plough again, because the vegetables go so deep into the ground, especially if they're big, that it's very costly and unproductive to dig them up one by one with a hoe or a spade. So, the day of the harvest, I harnessed the animal to the plough and, no sooner had I passed over the first plants than the upper part of a bulb appeared, leaning to one side, greeting the day. I snatched it with both hands and pulled hard, since it was still clinging to the soil; I pulled so energetically that when the fruit came out I fell backwards, my rear end hitting the ground and

remaining in that position. Anyone who saw me from afar, sitting down and embracing a whitish bulb from which I was removing soil and other things that had got stuck to it, caressing it and spilling tears of joy, would think they were watching someone cradling a new-born baby.

28. The day of our false wedding, in a ramshackle French chapel, was one of the most beautiful in my life. We were blessed by a short-sighted priest. Odra said to me: 'I will never be far from you; we will be like the vine and the soil.'

29. It was Odra who chose my name. 'It must start with R, like your name, so that we don't get it wrong, because it will be hard to remember to start with. And we will have to call you that forever, both in public and in private, to get used to it as soon as possible. We must forget your old form. Your new name must be short, like the one your mother gave me. And besides that...' *Besides what? Does it have to mean something?* 'Not really, we're looking for a name that refers only to you, that only signifies you, that distinguishes you from everyone else.' And then, that smile, as she imagined my definitive alias, looking at me, wondering which would suit me best, and I completely certain, looking at her illuminated face, that it was she who most suited me.

30. It was a chaotically beautiful afternoon; in the distance, on the other side of the Oder in the New March, it was raining, but a blinding sun kept Jakob and me comfortably sitting on some chairs in front of my house, just twelve metres from where I write

now; it was autumn, since I remember leaves on the ground and a somewhat crepuscular atmosphere, like the end of the world. Jakob was smoking his best pipe and talking about the Oder, its history, course and span, enumerating the towns that have used it as a canal, transport, a border and a space for warfare. It was then that I told him, with the casualness of the ignoramus, the innocent, who knows nothing and therefore dares to speak: *Jakob, I have sometimes seen flags and military standard flowing down these waters: the remains of skirmishes. Bodies too; bodies other than those that surround us have travelled down it, like monstrous fish. What if the Oder were not a river but a lesson, something we must interpret?* 'Oderbuch,' Jakob responded, punning on the region's name.[6] 'The Book of the Oder, where the true story of Europe can be read. And this parcel of land is the macabre footnote to that river and that book, Redo, the gloss where the bodies form a pool. Yes, you might well be right; history filled this earth with the silt of its abundant dead, those it did not want to carry out to sea, so that they would serve as a lesson for us.' *Do you think we will learn it, Jakob?* Jakob made a meaningful arm movement, pointing with his pipe at the enormous fence surrounding us on all sides, and responded: 'Does it look like we're learning anything?' *There will be more dead in the Oder, then.*

---

6 Oderbruch is the name of the region surrounding Frankfurt von Oder; in German *Oder,* as besides the homonymous river, means '*or*', hinting at the idea of choice; *Buch* means book; and *Bruch* has three meanings: *crack*, *piece* or *fragment* and mathematical *fraction*. (Translator's note)

'There will. You don't need to be Ilse to know that.' And we stayed there, looking at the silver of the river running northwards, so bright, so terrible, so dark, so light, so full of shadows.

31. I don't know how much time I have left, I suppose a few more years. I am proud of everything I have achieved. I changed my life, yes, and achieved much of what I set out to do. I have a reasonable and growing patrimony. I possess in practice a monopoly on all the sugar beet in the Oderbruch. Fourteen people now work with me or for me part-time, in fields of which they are co-owners, giving me a portion, with more than fair deals. Good friends make my life a joy: Hans, Wiesława, Johanna. I keep correspondence with some of the sharpest minds in Prussia and Austria, and I will not rule out beginning to write regularly for some Berlin newspaper about current affairs, in one of the *feuilletons* which *La Presse Parisienne* has made popular. I think I already have sufficient mental fluidity and literary skill to take the plunge. And I believe I also have things to say. Another division has been added to the double life I always played out with ease: I am a commercial producer for the people of Szonden and an intellectual one for those further away.

32. Yes, I'm going to do it, because all is well, because I do not have to give any more explanations, because nothing matters to me anymore. I've earned the right to be utterly free. To behave how I like once and for all. The coming years will play out as I see fit, in my way, I am going to live them with all the consequences. With no

more lies or fabrications. No more disguises. The time is approaching for everyone to know that I've done the most difficult things, lived without fear, filled the king of Prussia's boots with mud, left behind ignominy and ignorance, have rebuilt myself, changing some things in order to be another person: a complete person. Those young, frozen soldiers who remain upright in my field repeat their valuable lesson to me every day: live for now, Redo, one day you will be dead like us, don't resign yourself to a lesser life than the one you desire. That day someone will find me, they'll call a doctor, examine me, lift their hands to their head, strip me naked, they won't believe it, they'll find the envelope that's been lying over the chimney for months, addressed to the Lebus judge, who will open it, read my will and then, finally, run his eyes over my last wish regarding my own body: *Last of all, I ask that I be buried in my own living room, ten feet underground, with my dear Odra, in the same coffin, so that we can accompany one another for all eternity, far from the expectations of others, from any trace of the wards, far from ice and blood, together with my wife, in the heart of Europe.*